CLOCKWORK UNIVERSE
A STEAMPUNK THRILLER
JOHN W. DENNEHY

SEVERED PRESS
HOBART

CLOCKWORK UNIVERSE

WWW.SEVEREDPRESS.COM

ISBN: 978-1-925493-99-3

CHAPTER ONE

Sarah shivered from an early autumn chill as she trod up Park Street towards her family Brownstone. An ominous feeling of dread crept over her along with the brisk weather. The evening seemed grim and lonely. She pulled up the collar of her Victorian dress in an effort to ward off the cold.

Gas lanterns cast an intermittent glow from occasional lampposts, making the sidewalk appear desolate. A cacophony of sounds emanated from nearby Tremont Street. The noises were comforting when she had plied her way through the major thoroughfare. Steam buggies honked and revelers traipsing to taverns bellowed. Now, the distant clamor made her trek seem all the more isolated, and frightening.

She took a deep breath and grabbed hold of her billowing dress, pulling it above the ground in order to free her laced-up boots. Then, she huffed and picked up her pace, trotting down the brick sidewalk.

Boston Common lay below, an expansive public park boxed in by Park Street and Tremont Street. At night, the park appeared eerie, with the bare branches of tall, dark trees rattling in slight gusts of wind.

She sought to avoid the park, being careful to take the long way around it. The park had become the scene of grisly murders. Now, she felt even more vulnerable than she'd likely experience walking directly through the common.

A harsh noise suddenly caught her attention. Sarah came to a halt at the sound of metal creaking. Her pulse quickened, and her heart pounded. The thought of becoming the next victim consumed her, while fear drained her resolve, and paralysis locked her feet in place.

Then, the familiar clopping of hooves set her at ease. A moment later, a Hansom Cab rounded the curb and rolled over the cobblestone street. The driver nodded from his perch, and Sarah smiled in return; her trepidation slipped away as a grin appeared on her face.

She watched the horse-drawn buggy plod uphill, and then it turned a corner and slipped out of sight. The clip-clopping faded, leaving her alone once again.

The street fell silent, except for the repeated clicking of her heels. Sarah picked up her stride, and the sound of her boots muffled any other noise. Not much chance she'd hear someone approach from behind her. She slowed her pace and listened intently.

A footfall reverberated from the shadows. Sarah couldn't be certain whether it was a traveler, or a steam pipe coming to life in a nearby apartment.

She slackened her gait, and her hearing became more alert.

The unmistakable sound of a leather sole smacked the brick, and then repeated as though someone was walking nearby. She eased her pace further, and the stalker followed suit, matching her stride, as if trying to mask his steps with hers.

Sarah came to an abrupt halt.

The footsteps broke off, confirming her suspicion.

"Who's there?" Sarah said, defiantly.

No answer followed.

"Tell me who's there," Sarah repeated, "or you'll be sorry."

"Just a weary passerby," said a man after a moment.

"Show yourself," she demanded.

A scrawny man stepped from the shadows of an alleyway. He wore a tattered top hat and dusty overcoat. She discerned his bloodshot eyes in the flickering light of a gas lantern fixed to the façade of a brick apartment building.

He forced a smile, but his jowls still drooped. The man shuffled closer, displaying decayed teeth, yellowed and black.

Sarah could smell booze on his breath from four feet away. Liquor and body odor wafted through the cool air. The wretched man was detestable. A desire to kick him in the crotch and flee overwhelmed her. He stared at her too long without saying a word, a creepy desire lingered in his slovenly eyes. The urge to bolt consumed her thoughts.

"Tell me what you want," Sarah pressed.

"Wondering if you can spare a few pounds," he replied.

"Not sure you can be trusted," Sarah said, "stalking me and all."

"How about a few shillings, then?"

Sarah shook her head.

He trundled forward, staggering completely out of the alley. The filth became more palpable and his stench reeked something fierce.

"Afraid I cannot help you," she said, flatly.

"Won't you consider helping out… a wayward barrister in some need?"

"You shouldn't creep up on people like that," she snapped.

"My apologies." He forced an untrustworthy smile. "Didn't want to alarm you is all. Seemed to have done so anyway… just a few shillings and I'd be on my way."

Sarah figured the moment she reached into her purse, he'd pounce and filch everything of value. The bum would bang her up good in the process. "Sorry, but I must get going now," she finally said, and began to turn away.

He shuffled half a step forward, and that's when Sarah realized her mistake.

A set of beady eyes gleamed at her through the shimmering light, totally devoid of reason, and lacking compassion. The beggar's abject poverty had detached him from humanity. Sarah cringed and contemplated acquiescing to his demands.

She reached for her purse, slung over a shoulder. His eyes lit up in anticipation. Then, he leaned closer and licked his lips, wetting them with his tongue. An expectation of a drink consumed him. Sarah noticed him slip a hand into his trouser pocket, and registered her mistake in trusting him immediately.

The movement caused her to take a step back.

With a swift motion of his hand, a knife handle came into view. A click resonated in the night, and then a metallic blade reflected in the lamplight.

Sarah's muscles grew tense; her senses intensified, becoming more acute.

Her mind instantly registered that flight was not an option. She would have to fight the bastard. Sarah hurled a boot upward. The blow missed his groin and struck her attacker in the gut. He keeled over and let out a groan.

Then, she grabbed the handle of her purse, and swung the bag roundhouse into his head.

Sarah's handbag cracked into his pate and sent him stumbling backward. He bellowed in pain, reaching for his head. A confused look crossed his face.

The brick walkway reverberated from a heavy thud in the alleyway.

A menacing claw latched onto the beggar's shoulder. Long talons shredded his top coat and cleaved into his skin. Blood squirted in the air as he screamed in agony. Terror now registered in his former predatory eyes.

An effortless yank of the massive paw, and her attacker whisked out of sight.

Sarah heard the shrill wailing of his screams as she fled up the sidewalk. His shrieks abruptly cut off, leaving only a horrific, deafening silence. Then, the ground began to thunder behind her.

CHAPTER TWO

Kevin stood on the railway platform in a contemporary world, waiting for an ordinary commuter train into Boston, and he didn't have a care in the world. Although he considered his life boring, a real drag, he never contemplated it could turn for the better, more exciting, or sink into something much worse.

People glanced at him quickly and moved away. They pretended not to notice him in obvious ways. Most were professionals from the Merrimack Valley and southern New Hampshire, making the daily commute to North Station.

He played in a throwback punk band. Kevin liked to think the purple Mohawk, or oversized diaper pins in his ears, drove them off, but it was probably the jackboots with crimson laces.

Sprinkling raindrops stippled the platform and parking lot. Then, a deluge broke and cascaded buckets of precipitation. Kevin stepped under the overhang of the remote train station.

While everyone waited like drones, staring blankly at the tracks, he pumped to a shuffle that he'd loaded into his iPod: Sex Pistols, Dead Kennedys, and vintage Suicidal Tendencies.

A slender man wearing a black suit, white shirt, and narrow black tie approached him. The man had a grey trench coat draped over his arm, and carried a chrome attaché in the other hand.

Not paying the professional commuters any mind, Kevin didn't really notice the suit until the guy tapped him on the shoulder.

Kevin looked over at the man, perplexed.

"Like your jacket," the man said, putting the briefcase down.

"Thanks," Kevin said, and lowered the volume on his iPod. Kevin wore a black leather motorcycle jacket. Words painted on the back read: Punk's Not Dead, Just Dead Drunk. And there was a Dead Kennedys pin on the front.

"Used to be a big DK fan, myself," the man said to Kevin.

The suit looked to be in his mid-forties, and so he was ripe for their tours.

"Ever see them in concert?" Kevin asked.

"Sure, got to see them in Manhattan, actually."

"Wow," Kevin said. "What about the Sex Pistols, ever see them?"

"Saw them in Manhattan too."

"You're pulling my chain."

The man leaned forward, tilting his head slightly toward Kevin. At first, it seemed like the guy was acting strange. Then, Kevin saw the holes in his ears; he was for real. The man straightened up, grinning.

"You doubted me," the man said. "That's fine. You shouldn't trust establishment types... not at your age anyway."

Kevin laughed at the comment.

"By the way," he said, reaching for a handshake, "my name is Roland."

Kevin shook his hand.

"Do me a favor?" Roland said.

"Sure, what are you thinking?"

"Just watch my briefcase for a minute," Roland said. "I'll be right back."

"Sure thing."

Kevin watched as Roland donned his trench coat, and then stepped away from the kiosk. Roland hustled through the parking lot, rain dancing off car windshields, as though he'd forgotten something.

Waiting for ten minutes, Kevin started jonesing for a joint, or a lude. Anything but babysitting some yuppie's briefcase. Kevin scanned the parking lot, but he didn't see Roland anywhere.

Screeching rims signaled the train approaching. It was silver with a purple stripe running down the side; soot and grime dulled the metal cars.

The train came to a screeching halt, then passenger car doors creaked opened. Conductors alighted from the train wearing polyester blue uniforms. The uniforms had yellow trim on the cuffs and jacket seams; their round hats had short visors, and the same yellow trim ran around the top of each hat.

Haverhill was the end of the line, making it the first stop going inbound, so no passengers alighted from the train. After placing portable steps on the ground at most every door, the conductors ushered people onto the train. The conductors moved about in haste, as the train had a schedule to keep, and wouldn't wait for anyone.

Kevin looked around and still didn't see any sign of Roland.

Everyone rushed to the train, appearing fearful of missing it, and then having to wait an hour for the next departure. Nobody paid any mind to Kevin, and so he snagged the chrome attaché and climbed aboard the train.

Walking down the aisle, Kevin found many seats available. He wanted to face forward and walked past the seats pointed at the rear of the train. The seats were large, dark vinyl, cheap imitation leather. On the left side of the train, there were rows of two seats, but the opposite side had three seats together.

Figuring the train would fill up closer to Boston, Kevin opted for a window in a two-seater. He set the briefcase down beside him, expecting Roland to come strolling down the aisle.

The conductors scrambled onto the train, holding the portable steps. As they stowed the steps away, the train began to slowly churn forward.

****

While the train jostled along, people continued to meander down the aisle looking for seats, but Roland wasn't one of them. Kevin hoped the briefcase would deter people from sitting next to him. And maybe Roland would come along and spot it.

Kevin stuffed his ticket under a flap on the seat in front of him. He curled against the window and closed his eyes, trying to fall asleep.

The conductors came by punching tickets. Although they didn't bother Kevin, a conductor reached across and punched his ticket; there was enough disruption that he couldn't fall entirely asleep.

Soon, the train was making stops and filling up with boarders. Kevin heard a conductor arguing with a passenger.

"You can't ride the train without a ticket," the conductor said.

"Well, I haven't got a ticket."

"You either need a ticket," the conductor said, "or the funds to pay for your ride."

The man sat a few rows up from Kevin. He was disheveled with a sullen, plump face. He wore a soiled white t-shirt and khakis splattered by paint. A tall conductor with a haggard countenance stood lurching over the man; he called for assistance. Then, a burly conductor joined him and they accosted the interloper.

No longer checking people's tickets as the train sailed along, they only focused on the freeloader. They seemed to believe he had the means to pay the fare, but wanted to try riding for free.

"Are you going to pay, or what?" the tall conductor snapped, pale jowls bobbing.

"Listen, I don't have the money."

"Well, then you're going to have to get off the train."

"What?"

"We'll let you ride to the next stop, and we'll kindly let you off. We won't charge you for the ride you've taken," the conductor said. "But you've got to agree to it now. Otherwise, we'll call ahead and have the police waiting for you."

"That's fine," the man said. "I'll get off at the next stop. Alright?"

"No trouble?"

"None."

The conductors left him and went about their business.

A moment later, the taller one approached Kevin. "Sorry lad, but you're going to have to put that in the overhead," he said, pointing at the attaché. "We've got more passengers getting on. There won't be an empty seat when we pull into North Station."

Reaching for the attaché, Kevin grabbed it with both hands. He noticed the case felt warm.

A cool, damp autumn day, and the train car had begun heating up, so he didn't think much about it. Looking up, Kevin noticed the overhead appeared quite full, so he put the briefcase on the floor between his leg and the outside wall. He leaned back and cranked up the volume on his iPod.

At the next stop, the conductors ushered the freeloader off the train. More passengers climbed aboard and then a young, petite brunette with shoulder-length hair stopped near Kevin. She wore a black pantsuit and a blue blouse. Leaning over, she spoke to Kevin, but he couldn't hear her.

Kevin turned the music down.

"Is anyone sitting here?" she said, pointing to the empty seat.

"No," he said, shaking his head. "It's all yours."

She sat down, placing her handbag on the floor. For some reason, this young woman didn't seem taken aback by Kevin. He pondered whether he was losing his edge. Usually only girls with tats talked to him, not strait-laced girls like this.

"Where are you headed?" she asked.

"Just into town," he said. "Trying to get a gig for my band."

"Got anything good lined up?"

"Hoping for an opening at the Orpheum for Suicidal Tendencies," he said. "They're making a comeback tour this fall."

"Sounds cool."

"And you?" he said. "Where are you headed?"

"Just to the office," she replied.

"What do you do?" he asked.

"Public relations," she said, tilting her head. She stuck out her tongue and pointed at it. "Yuk."

"Nothing wrong with a good sit," Kevin said. "A steady income pays the bills."

She nodded. "But it's boring."

"Things will change up, eventually," he said. "I'm Kevin by the way, Kevin Barnes."

"Sarah," she said, with a quick grin. Then she turned her attention to fishing something from her handbag.

As the train hummed along, Sarah turned on a small laptop and shoved in a pair of earbuds; the cord ran to her phone. Kevin heard the distinct sound of Marilyn Manson and understood why she'd been so approachable.

He leaned against the side of the train car and drifted off to sleep.

CHAPTER THREE

The sound of screeching steel rims, along with the momentum of a braking train, jerked Kevin forward, and jostled him awake.

A conductor quickly moved down the aisle. It was the tall conductor who had accosted the freeloader, except he'd changed his clothing. Now, he wore a grey uniform, tailored from high quality wool, the edges of the uniform and cap were trimmed in black.

The conductor's face looked fresher; the time-worn fatigue was gone, and he had a spring in his step.

Adjusting himself in the large seat, Kevin realized that it seemed plusher, the vinyl felt softer, like cowhide.

He looked over at Sarah to find her wearing a long black dress that flared at the hip. The mid-section was crimson with a row of large buttons running down the front. She busied herself on a laptop, but it was encased in polished mahogany and trimmed in fine brass.

Kevin glanced around and noticed that everyone seemed dressed in outdated clothes. He felt a tinge of panic, and fought to gulp down bile that had risen in his throat.

Another conductor walked past and he was also wearing a grey, wool uniform.

A boisterous man across the aisle, a few seats up, caught Kevin's attention. The man was large and talking to someone seated across the aisle. The big man wore a shooting jacket and had a thick, walrus mustache. His chubby red face tilted up and down habitually, as he listened to a slender man, seemingly in agreement with what the big fellow was saying.

But the big man's dark, squinty eyes didn't reveal his actual position. Kevin heard the slender man talking, but couldn't make everything out, and then the conversation ticked up a bit.

"Sure, it's a serious situation," the big man agreed.

"Sounds like they're taking the right precautions."

"The 10th Royal Hussars have been deployed to Boston," the big man explained.

"Excellent," the man said, adjusting his spectacles. "I'm sure they'll have things under control forthwith."

"Afraid not." The big man disagreed.

"Why the heavens not?"

"This really isn't a military exercise," the big man said.

"Oh."

"It is more of a hunt."

"I see," the slender man intimated. "And you don't think that the 10th are up to the task."

"They are a fine outfit," the big man said. "But for something like this, you need a big game hunter."

"Someone like you?"

"Certainly, that's why the Honorable East India Company retained my services."

"So, I guess you'll have the chance to be a big hero."

"Not after heroics," the big man chuckled. "Just here to do my job. A job that I must point out came recommended by the Corps of Royal British Engineers."

"That so," the man said. "Interesting, very interesting indeed. Why, you must know some important people."

"Not at all, my good man."

"Really?"

"There were some concerns that the beasts had gotten into the infrastructure around Boston," the big man explained. "Someone got the notion that it will take a hunter to track them down."

The man across the aisle nodded, seeming to follow along. "And how exactly did you come to be involved?" he said.

"They decided to put together a list of the top five big game hunters."

"And you were number one?"

"Heavens no," the big man cackled. "The top four were all too busy."

The slender man smiled at the joke, and then nervously adjusted his glasses.

Reaching over, still grinning, the big man smacked the slender man on the shoulder. "The top four were busy," he repeated, continuing to chuckle at the joke.

Kevin didn't understand the discussion. At first, he considered why the British would have any interest in the local affairs of Boston, and then he glanced around at how everyone was dressed. He pondered if the discussion were merely part of a charade.

Wondering if people on the train had changed clothes while he slept, perhaps participating in a sort of costume event, Kevin's attention was diverted to the slowing train. He could feel the chugging, mechanical spurts, far smoother than when it had departed from Haverhill and other stops along the way.

A stream of sooty, black smoke whisked by his window. The train continued to lunge forward, as the locomotive churned steel rims over iron rails; an occasional sleeper gave way under the weight of the train, jostling the passengers, and then heaps of smoke rhythmically released in unison with the engine's forward progress.

Leaning toward Sarah, he lightly tapped her shoulder. "Did we change trains while I was asleep?"

"Don't be silly, Mr. Barnes," she responded, rolling her eyes. Sarah smiled and then turned back to her computer, which hummed and spit as she worked the odd keyboard.

Kevin felt another twinge of panic race through his veins.

He saw the tall conductor headed his way.

"What's going on?" Kevin asked.

"Headed into North Station," the conductor replied, matter-of-factly. His countenance didn't reveal any concern whatsoever, but Kevin didn't breathe any more easily.

****

When the train slowed, everything seemed like business as usual to the other passengers.

Kevin glanced out the window. A huge water tower lingered over the outbound tracks. Although he'd never seen it before on his trips into the city, the tower didn't appear to be new construction. Beads of rust ran from the rim of the cistern, and thick soot coated the fill-pipe.

Beyond the water tower, an immense platform jutted toward the track. Prodigious heaps of coal mounded on broad planks, turned grey from coal dust. The platform abutted a small building. Shovels were pegged on the façade, and a sign hung over the door, reading: East India Company Line.

Kevin shook his head in disbelief. He had a sinking feeling, as anxiety and panic swept over him.

As the train eased into the station, passengers rose from their seats. Sarah deposited her laptop into a leather satchel, which zipped closed like a doctor's bag. Then, she stood in the aisle, and tossed the bag over her shoulder. She reached for a bonnet from the overhead.

Others packed up and pressed into the crowded aisle. Kevin noticed most passengers wore Victorian garments. He wondered again if there was a costume event. He decided to sit tight and wait for the passageway to clear out.

The train lurched to a halt.

A moment later, car doors creaked open, and cool air rushed inside. Conductors assisted passengers alighting from the train. Although people swarmed out to the platform, the aisle remained jam-packed. Many people fiddled with their belongings. Kevin noticed Sarah holding things up.

"Well, Mr. Barnes," she said, patting down the sides of her dress. "Aren't you going to escort a lady off the train?"

He stood up quickly and reached for the attaché. But instead of grabbing hold of a smooth metal handle, his grasp lay on comfortable leather. Looking down in shock, Kevin saw the briefcase was now an old leather portmanteau.

"Hurry it up, Mr. Barnes," Sarah barked. "You're holding up the line."

"Sorry," he replied. "Sorry, miss."

Kevin nervously scurried into the aisle, and while doing so, caught a grin on Sarah's face as she impatiently stood by.

"My, what has gotten into you, Mr. Barnes," she said, mischievously. "Suddenly all bashful. Where's that confident young man I met?"

Trying to figure out what's going on, he thought.

They stepped onto the platform and followed a herd of people headed into North Station. A group of passengers walked in the opposite direction beyond a row of columns. They were similarly dressed to the people getting off of his train. Everyone wore extraordinary Victorian garb, or wool suits from the early 1900s, except Kevin.

He glanced at the passengers boarding the outbound train, and spied the magnificent locomotive. An enormous black engine with a smoke stack, it had a large cylindrical boiler. Prodigious bolts protruded from the engine, and the locomotive had large steel wagon wheels, painted black like the engine, joined by a shiny metal bar. Behind the engine, a car overflowed with shiny chunks of coal; and following the coal car were a number of ornate passenger cars. The thick metal cars were painted red. And the windows were all ornamented by plush curtains. The antiquated train was pristine and looked new.

Glancing back at the train he'd disembarked from, Kevin noticed it was as grand as the one people were boarding nearby. He found the trains unsettling. It was easy to comprehend a bunch of people gathering for a costume event, but swapping out the dilapidated silver commuter cars for posh steam trains seemed a little over the top.

Walking along the platform with Sarah by his side, Kevin gently swung the portmanteau, ever so slightly, marking the cadence of each step.

Most of the passengers got off the train and traipsed toward North Station, but a few were unloading belongings from the storage compartment underneath the train. The doors to the bays were levered open, revealing the belly of each car beneath the posh travel compartments. Steam trunks, leather suitcases, and oversized leather bags were hauled onto the platform.

Kevin and Sarah confronted a pile of baggage blocking their path. They went to move around the obstacle when the big man with the walrus mustache stopped them.

"Do you mind lending me a hand?" he said to Kevin, a tone of official business.

"What do you need, sir?" Kevin replied, diffident.

"Just some help getting my belongings through the station," the big man replied. "I have a ride waiting."

"Sure, sure thing." Kevin didn't understand this strange environment, so he just went along with the customs, trying not to upset anyone.

"Much obliged," the big man said. "I'm Silas Cunningham."

"Kevin Barnes."

They shook hands.

"And this is my friend, Sarah," Kevin added.

"Glad to meet your acquaintance," Cunningham said, slightly bending forward. He held a safari hat in hand.

Cunningham seemed to notice Kevin's clothing for the first time. And Kevin observed Cunningham's safari hunting outfit; his shooting jacket had a brown recoil pad on the right shoulder. Cunningham also wore safari pants and brown boots, laced almost to the knee.

They stood there for a moment looking each other over.

"I'm a big game hunter," Cunningham explained. "There are a couple of monstrous animals on the loose, ravishing the city."

Kevin nodded, understanding the outfit, but the comment sent a chill down his spine. *Monsters.* He found himself in a strange world and pictured giant killer beasts taking buildings down. A daunting thought.

"What about you?" Cunningham said after a moment. "By the look of your outfit and that hairdo, I'd say that you've just returned from the Orient."

Kevin shook his head.

"Where do you hail from?"

"New Hampshire," Kevin answered. "Just over the border."

"A fine colony," Cunningham said, bending over to grab a few bags. "But you've certainly been to the Far East. Seen others that have gotten bitten by that culture."

Kevin thought the comment presumptuous, but didn't pay it much mind. "So, what do you need?" he asked.

"These here bags are mine," Cunningham said, pointing.

Kevin grabbed hold of a steam trunk fitted with wheels. He noticed the wheels were attached to the trunk with fine brass hardware. With his free hand, he hefted a long wooden box, and grasped it tightly along with his portmanteau.

"Be careful with that one there," Cunningham said. "It's holding my Weatherby .460 and a Springfield thirty-ought-six."

Kevin looked at him wide-eyed, thinking about gun laws in Massachusetts.

"What troubles you, my lad?"

"Do you have a license for bringing guns into the city?" Kevin said.

"License?" Cunningham retorted, shaking his head. "Never heard of such a thing. Sounds like some sort of plutocratic restriction."

"Well, I am not comfortable with—"

Sarah placed a hand on Kevin's shoulder. "Sorry to trouble you, sir. My friend seems to enjoy a lecture, but we're happy to help with your belongings. What can I carry?"

A scowl slipped away from Cunningham's face. "This bag here should do it," he said, pointing at a burlap duffle bag.

She smiled and heaved the duffle bag over her shoulder. Cunningham turned toward North Station and plodded along the platform. The hunter quickly pulled ahead of them. Kevin was busy jockeying the large steam trunk, portmanteau, and long wooden rifle case, while Sarah got weighed down by her small workbag and Cunningham's travel bag.

Kevin looked at her and shook his head.

"What is it with you... Barnes?" Sarah said.

"We could get into trouble for carrying unlicensed weapons in the city," he said. "And I'm not keen on getting arrested."

"The only thing requiring a license is the practice of law, and running a saloon."

He looked at her perplexed.

"Just tote the bags and be a *nice* boy."

"I'm not a boy."

"Have you served overseas?" said Sarah. "The older generation tends to mark a man by his service. Quite sure that you'll find Mr. Cunningham was once in the Army."

"Not so sure that I agree with your position," Kevin said, straining to haul the trunk and rifle case. "What about artists, writers, and poets?"

"The greatest poets came out of service in the Great War."

He shook his head, defeated.

They continued along, falling further behind Cunningham as the hunter pressed forward. People tended to clear the way as he approached, barreling along; his immense bulk cast shadows over passengers headed into the station.

The doors to the station were propped open, and the window panes were painted dark green.

Stepping inside the station, Kevin barely recognized the building. He watched as sundry travelers traipsed across the shiny plank flooring; the hems of intricate gowns skimmed over the wooden floor. Men wore tightly tailored suits, many of which had tailcoats. Most everyone carried a hat or bonnet; others who had their hands full with luggage took the burden as legitimate reason to don their hat. The station seemed to be an extension of outdoors, unlike entering a professional office or church.

Kevin's heart fluttered from fear of what was going on. The charade seemed far too elaborate, and so he began to wonder if he'd lost this mind.

Wooden benches were set around the station. Along the far wall, ticket windows protruded above oak-paneled walls. Nowhere did Kevin discern the remnants of the modern station he had come to know. The cement floor covered in commercial tile, replaced by polished hardwood; plastic trashcans swapped with mesh wire baskets, and the drop-down ceiling with foam panels had changed to cherry bead-board. And the walls were painted in a light, misty green, appearing dense as though constructed from plaster and lathe.

Trailing Cunningham through the station, Kevin wondered if he was having a complete mental breakdown. Anxiety consumed him, and he broke out in a sweat. The entire experience from the time he'd awoken on the train was surreal. It didn't seem to register with anyone else. Stepping through another set of double French doors, Kevin felt the cool autumn air whisk over him.

CHAPTER FOUR

Outside, the sun shined bright and people ambled about their business. The first thing Kevin noticed was the dirt road, congested with work wagons slowly moving down the street in either direction, each wagon being pulled by a dray horse.

Some of the wagons were flatbeds, loaded with supplies and provisions. Others were enclosed, similar to the wagons peddlers used in the old west, except these were stenciled with the names of local businesses. A wagon hauled newspapers, and another brought ice to customers around the city.

A steam lorry made its way down the road. It was a cross between a steam locomotive and stake-bed truck, with a cylindrical boiler and smoke stack on the front, and a long flatbed with fixed rails on the back. The driver's compartment resembled a pickup truck, only driven on oversized steel wheels.

Some wealthier folks headed to the curb from the train station, climbing into Hansom Cabs drawn by stout thoroughbred horses. Kevin noticed an occasional steam buggy bop along the road, two-seaters mostly, because the rear served for coal storage.

The steam buggies resembled early Ford Model-A automobiles, equipped with seats propped high above the floorboards. They had big wagon wheels encased in thick rubber. Oversized fenders covered each wheel to help prevent mud from caking the passengers. Each steam car was adorned with brass lamps, a brass steering wheel, and rich leather seats.

Kevin felt beside himself viewing the scene outside North Station. His heart pounded from anxiety, and, despite the brisk weather, he suddenly felt extremely hot, almost feverish.

Shock had settled in, and his stomach churned. He felt like throwing up.

Taking a deep breath, Kevin noticed Sarah plugging along beside him. She seemed content, smiling pleasantly. Cunningham barreled down the sidewalk, intent on his destination without losing a moment.

The destination appeared to be a vehicle parked farther down the curb. As Cunningham approached, the driver got out and waved. He was also dressed in safari garb. The vehicle resembled a Range Rover, except for the roof rack, loaded with a coal bin. The rear storage compartment appeared to house an apparatus for burning coal, and a hot water tank, and then piping led to the steam engine under the hood.

A spare tire was fastened to the hood, and a small exhaust pipe jutted through the center of the wheel. The vehicle rumbled, idling curbside. Puffs of black smoke emanated from the little pipe.

Hurrying over to Cunningham, the driver grabbed a bag from him, and then headed back to the Rover. He opened the back door and shoved the bag inside. Cunningham tossed his luggage into the vehicle and turned back up the sidewalk.

Even though Sarah handled her baggage well, and Kevin struggled with three items, Cunningham relieved her of the burlap duffle bag. He placed it on the seat. Then, Cunningham waited by the door for Kevin to hurry it up. When Kevin reached the Rover, Cunningham took the rifle case and gently placed it inside. Then the two hunters hoisted the steam trunk onto the roof.

Cunningham tipped his hat to Sarah, and then reached out to Kevin.

Kevin shook the hunter's meaty hand.

"Much obliged," Cunningham said.

"No problem."

"By the way, this is my colleague Niles Barton," he said, pointing.

Niles smiled and nodded.

"Can we repay your gratitude… by giving you a lift?" Niles said.

Sarah and Kevin looked at each other.

"Where are you headed?" she asked Cunningham.

"My quarters are up on Beacon Hill, I'm told."

"Not far from my parent's house," Sarah said. "We would love to join you. In fact, we'll help you unload."

Cunningham grinned widely. "Why, you certainly have the *absolute* manners of a lady."

"Is there room for us?" Kevin asked. "I mean with the baggage and all."

"You're not all that big, young man," Cunningham quipped.

Niles smirked at the comment. "Let me arrange things back there, and the two of you can squeeze in."

As Niles busied himself adjusting the luggage, Kevin took another look around. He checked for signs of the city as he knew it. The streets appeared to be laid out the same, only dirt or cobblestone. Scanning the buildings in the distance, the brick and limestone office buildings seemed the same. He couldn't quite place what was different, but something was extremely peculiar.

"All set," Niles said, stepping around to the front door.

Niles slid behind the wheel next to Cunningham. A rear door was left open with bags shoved against the opposite side. Kevin looked at Sarah perplexed as to what they should do.

She seemed to pick up on the conundrum. "Typically, you would assist a lady into a coach, and then climb in after her. However, difficult situations call for the most chivalrous steps to be taken."

"Which seating would you prefer?" he said.

Sarah smiled widely. "A gentleman should bear the discomfort, rather than a lady. As for me, I'm quite capable of boarding this motor coach myself."

Kevin started climbing into the back when he felt a gentle tap on the shoulder. Turning, he saw Sarah handing him her bag. He climbed in and sat squished against the luggage with the portmanteau and Sarah's bag both on his lap.

Delicately slipping onto the back seat, Sarah smiled and then shut the door with a reverberating echo. The sound demonstrated intense physical strength lurking beneath her elegant dress.

CHAPTER FIVE

Niles drove the Rover through dense traffic, cutting around slow moving dray horses pulling wagons. Further away from North Station, the city revealed more of the same misgivings: dirt roads, steam buggies, and wagons, as well as people clad in Victorian attire.

Not a sole dressed in blue jeans or modern day fashion. Kevin had hoped what he witnessed on the train and at the station were merely part of an elaborate movie set. Such a prospect was dashed as the bizarre scenes extended further into the city. Then, he finally noticed what was strikingly different, aside from the carriages and dress. Kevin sunk into despair.

The old Custom House reigned over the city with its clock tower jutting above the skyline. All of the modern skyscrapers were missing. Kevin realized that he was somewhere completely different, a strange world, but he could not comprehend how it had happened.

As the Rover took a turn, Sarah swayed and pressed Kevin into the luggage. He gasped for air. The shock of his situation and claustrophobic quarters made it difficult to breathe. Kevin felt blood drain from his face.

The Rover straightened out and Sarah moved away. She seemed to sense that something was wrong. "Are you all right?" she inquired. "You look a little queasy, I dare say."

"Just need to catch my breath," Kevin replied.

"Have you ever been in a motor car before?" she said. "Perhaps it is making you sick. It is quite common for people to grow ill in motor cars, especially when they are new to the experience."

"This isn't my first ride. I've been in a lot of them."

"Well, what the devil is wrong with you then?"

"Just a little jam-packed in here. Makes it difficult to breathe."

Niles looked over his shoulder. "Should have opened the window," he said. "Tight fit back there, tight fit."

"Can't do it now," Kevin said. "The luggage is pressed against the crank."

"Well, I can get to mine," Sarah offered, cracking her window.

"Thanks."

"Is that better?" she said.

Kevin nodded. "Much better."

"Ole Niles was kind enough to pick us up," Cunningham blurted. "We all owe cheers to my comrade, Niles."

"Thank you, Niles," Kevin and Sarah said in unison.

"She's a smart one, boy," Cunningham added. "You should keep an eye on her."

Kevin canted his head.

Cunningham looked back at him and seemed to note the confusion. "What I mean," he explained, "is don't let her out of your sight."

"Why would you say that?" Kevin asked.

"Listen, young lad," Cunningham explained. "If she were my girl, I'd hold on to her damn tight. That's all that I'm saying."

"But she's not—"

Sarah's giggling cut off Kevin's response.

"That's what you think," Cunningham added. "So, where are you all traveling from? I'm coming straight down from Canada after a successful hunting trip."

"Just coming into the city from New Hampshire," Kevin replied.

"And I'm on my way home to my parent's house, after spending a few days with my auntie," Sarah said.

"Your parents live on Beacon Hill, correct?" Cunningham asked.

"That is precisely where they reside."

"Not far from our lodgings," Niles said. "We'll unload and then drive you home. Mr. Barnes, where are you going, certainly not right back to New Hampshire?"

Kevin sat there for a moment, uncertain as what to say. He'd been so caught up in trying to understand the monolithic changes that he hadn't begun to fathom how he fit into things.

"Pray tell, lad," Niles insisted. "Certainly, we can't be driving you up to New Hampshire. A fine colony, but we've got work to do."

Kevin pondered the question, but didn't have a response. He noticed Cunningham peering over the seat, looking at him suspiciously.

"Well, young man, let's have it," Cunningham finally said.

"You can just drop me on Tremont Street... somewhere convenient."

"Somewhere convenient?" Cunningham pondered. "How the blazes do we know what's convenient unless you tell us."

"I mean somewhere that's easy for you."

"Oh, right you are," Cunningham said, rubbing his walrus mustache. "Don't mean to pester you, son. But you do stand out as a bit odd. Are you in a fix?"

"Perhaps... I don't really know for certain yet."

"Well, maybe we can help," Cunningham suggested. "Being from New Hampshire, how familiar are you with the city?"

Kevin looked out the window and noticed that most of the streets and historic buildings were the same. He could walk blindfolded around Boston and find his way. "Quite well," he replied. "I attended a University here for a couple of years."

"A University man," Cunningham said enthusiastically.

Niles chuckled. "Silas and I are from England and served the British Empire together for many years."

"Niles was an officer," Cunningham explained. "Earned the rank of Major before taking retirement."

"And Silas was a Sergeant Major," Niles said.

"An enlisted man," Cunningham offered. "I worked for a living."

They both chuckled.

"Being from out of town," Cunningham said, "we could use a gun bearer."

"A sort of scout," Niles added.

Kevin considered the offer. He really had few options and began to fear being shut out in the cold with little money in his pocket. And then he wondered what type of currency would even pass in the city.

"There'll be a few pounds in it for you of course," Cunningham pressed.

"And some lodging," Niles said.

The proffered exploit and safe lodging were too good to resist. "Sure, I can help you out. But I have to check on… some business first."

"Right, right on," Cunningham said. "We have a deal then."

Sarah looked at Kevin and smiled. "Quite an adventure," she said. "And to be part of such a big hunt for the most dangerous creatures."

"Dangerous creatures?" Kevin repeated.

"Most certainly so," Sarah replied. "Absolutely the most dangerous creatures to have ever set foot in the New World. I barely escaped one of them myself."

****

Later, Kevin pondered what he had signed up to do, then the Rover pulled onto Tremont Street. They drove past historic churches and graveyards and turned at the corner of Boston Common. The entrance to Park Street Station stood intact.

Kevin noticed a sign on the side of the rectangular building just below the green corrugated metal roof.

Any semblance of subway transportation as he knew it was gone. The sign read: TROLLEY LINE, and included an elaborately carved steam trolley under the writing. Beneath the carving, it stated *Park Street Station* in flowing cursive.

Niles took a left at the top of Beacon Hill onto a cobblestone roadway. Turning in front of the Bulfinch State House, an immense Union Jack flew in front of the building. The rich blue and red flag, trimmed in crisp white, fluttered proudly in a cool breeze.

Kevin felt his stomach sinking.

The Rover had a firm suspension, sending the shock of the uneven roadway into his spine. Jostled by the bumpy road, and the sight of the British flag, caused Kevin to grow nauseous. He could barely survive in a feeble modern world, depending upon his parents to provide room and board, while he worked an assortment of gigs that barely earned drinking money. The thought of competing in a world full of so many able men and intelligent, capable, and proper women was daunting.

"You're looking pale again," Sarah said, lowering the window further.

"Thanks," Kevin said, breathing heavily to steady himself.

"We're almost there," Niles said.

Kevin felt a draft from the cool air, and took another deep breath. Sitting confined in the back of the Rover, he realized the portmanteau rest on his lap. It no longer radiated heat.

"There we are now," Niles said cheerily. He pointed to a large Brownstone looming over the cobblestone road.

"That looks like fine quarters indeed," Cunningham said. Turning to the passengers in back, he added, "Niles was kind enough to come in advance and secure our quarters. Haven't even been here yet. Took a detour up into Canada."

"Did you hit anything up there?" Kevin asked.

"Did I hit anything?" Cunningham repeated. "The Great Hunter always takes down big game, my dear chap. But we tend to leave the spoils to the clients most of the time."

"I think that I get it," Kevin said.

Niles turned the Rover down a brick alley and brought it to a halt.

"We can unload here," Niles said. "And leave the Rover parked off the main road. It's just a short walk around the corner."

They climbed out and divided up the bags. With Niles assisting, Kevin didn't have to handle the steam trunk. Cunningham headed toward the Brownstone in haste, while Niles followed behind him with the trunk.

Kevin followed after them, carrying the rifle case in one hand and the leather portmanteau in the other. He'd slung the burlap duffle bag over a shoulder. The trunk bobbled over the uneven sidewalk and bounced up the steps. Kevin's pulse raced, fearful and exhilarated at taking part in such a fantastic hunt.

CHAPTER SIX

Entering the Brownstone, Sarah walked into the foyer of an ornate dwelling. The ceilings were three or four meters high, trimmed in intricate millwork, carried over to the doorways, windows and baseboards. Oriental rugs covered polished hardwood floors. An archway opened into a large living room.

Cunningham stood in the living room beside his bags. Everyone followed suit and placed the luggage in a pile. The Great Hunter lingered in the middle of the room with both hands on his hips. He was barrel-chested; the shooting jacket stretched due to his girth.

"Take a seat," Cunningham said, waving a hand.

Sarah sat down on a comfortable flame-stitched Chippendale sofa. A tea table was in front of it. Wing chairs flanked the sofa and Niles took a seat in one of them. The room had a large fireplace and a wall of bookcases; a variety of paintings hung about the Brownstone and prodigious windows overlooked the street.

Keven stood in the doorway, nervously.

"Take a seat," Sarah said, motioning to a spot on the sofa beside her.

He forced a smile and sat down.

Cunningham paced about, familiarizing himself with his new lodgings. Watching Cunningham, Sarah noticed a dining room adjacent to the living room, just beyond a set of intricate columns.

Then, the big man sauntered into the hall, and headed toward, what she expected, was the kitchen. The boisterous sound of his voice carried down the hallway, seemingly a pleasant greeting.

He came back with a wide grin on his face. A middle-aged woman, wearing an apron, trailed after him. The woman looked them over nervously.

Cunningham stepped toward the tea table. "Would you care to take lunch with us?" he said to Sarah.

"Most certainly would be obliged," Sarah said. "Why thank you."

The middle-aged woman stepped beside Cunningham. "My apologies," she said. "I got busy at the sink… with the water running, and didn't hear you enter. May I get you some sandwiches and hot tea?"

Most everyone nodded.

"That would do perfectly well," Cunningham said, grinning.

"My name is Alice by the way, if any of you requires further assistance."

Alice turned and left the room. Cunningham seemed to peruse the quarters further, and then stepped over towards his gear. "Do you have any experience with firearms?" he said to Kevin, bending over the rifle case.

"Sure, I'm from New Hampshire."

"What does that mean, lad?" Niles asked.

"Most everyone up there lives in the country," Kevin explained. "And so, we grow up shooting skeet, target practice, and hunting."

Opening the rifle case, Cunningham carefully removed a rifle. He pointed it down at the floor and worked the bolt open, double-checking to ensure it wasn't loaded. "Ever see one of these?" he said.

Sarah watched Kevin peruse the large letter "W" stamped on the sling. The wooden stock was pristine and the barrel-bluing in excellent condition. She smelled the sweet scent of gun oil wafting through the living room. The stock had a rubber recoil with the word Weatherby written across it. A big bore elephant gun, she doubted the padded stock provided much benefit.

"Can't say that I have," Kevin finally admitted. "The only really big game that we have in New Hampshire is moose. And you have to go way up north to find them. We mostly shoot white-tailed deer."

Cunningham nodded. "Our business is about going after the biggest, most dangerous animals on earth," he said proudly, putting the stock into his shoulder. "And this is about the finest rifle for doing so."

"*That*… and the Gibbs," Niles said.

"And the Gibbs .505," Cunningham agreed.

"Tell them about your brush with death in Uganda."

"Well, if we're waiting for lunch," Cunningham said, grinning. "Niles and I, along with a few gun bearers, were positioned in the African brush. Our clients wanted trophies, but seemed squeamish about alighting from the Rover."

They all sat up with interest as Cunningham commanded the floor, holding the rifle and telling the story at the same time.

"Suddenly, out of the bush, came two water buffalo charging madly," he said, eyes bright with excitement. "Their horns swung fierce and wide. See, they must have been cooling off in the tall grass, and so we hadn't spotted them."

"They were about twenty meters away," Niles added.

"Yes, that's right," Cunningham confirmed. "Twenty meters away. Niles was right next to me. Only he didn't have a gun. It was just me and this Weatherby."

Cunningham knelt down, one knee on the floor, holding the rifle with his elbow cocked to the side, like he was about to shoot. "Those buffalo closed in fast. Their horns looking bigger and bigger. You could see the moisture on their noses. They were that close, and kicking up dust."

"Didn't know what to do at first," Niles commented.

"So, there I was with the rifle raised to shoot from a kneeling position," Cunningham said, acting it out. "The buffalo are closing in. Now, they were about fifteen meters away. Niles shouts, 'Hits 'em!'"

Niles nodded in agreement.

"So, I takes aim and shoots the lead buffalo in the shoulder," Cunningham said, holding the rifle and pretending to work the bolt. "But it only slows him. He's charging mad, see. And then Niles yells, 'Hits 'em again!' And now it's ten meters away. I shoot his other shoulder, and he drops."

"The other one continued to charge," Niles said, smiling.

"Right, the other one continued to charge, madly," Cunningham said, "head down ready to maul us with its horns. Then Niles bellows, 'Hits the other one!'"

Niles nodded, grinning.

"So, knowing how the buffalo has such a thick skull," Cunningham said, again pretending to work the bolt, discharging an imaginary casing and loading another round. "I wait until it's almost upon us. Then, I fired off a round with the Weatherby .460, right between its eyes."

"The buffalo continued to charge," Niles said, motioning with his hands. "And dropped dead, a meter in front of us."

Cunningham stood up with a wide grin, and hitched up his pants. He shook his head smiling, as though the near brush with death was mere nonsense.

The room fell quiet. Hearing the story, Sarah glanced over at Kevin. He had a solemn look on his face, as though realizing that these men were into a serious business.

****

Later, Alice returned holding a silver tray, loaded with sandwiches cut in half, a teapot, and four cups and saucers. She placed the serving tray on the tea table in front of Sarah.

"There you are," Alice said, turning to leave. "Please let me know if you need anything else."

"Looks fine," Cunningham remarked, reaching for a sandwich. "Looks mighty fine indeed."

Sarah took charge, filling the tea cups, as the rest of the men grabbed a sandwich.

"Thank you, kindly," Niles said, reaching for his tea.

"This tea is excellent," Sarah said, taking a delicate sip while holding out her pinky. She took a cloth napkin and placed it on her lap before biting into a sandwich.

Niles and Kevin followed her example, but only after she started to eat.

"Niles, these are exceptional lodgings," Cunningham said. "And the service is top-notch. You've outdone yourself this time."

"Don't thank me," Niles replied. "The Honorable East India Trading Company made all of the arrangements."

"Perhaps a side benefit of an assignment such as this."

"Expect they will get their monies worth."

"Suppose they will," Cunningham added, finally sitting down in the empty chair near Sarah. Half a sandwich already devoured, he reached for his spot of tea and gulped most of it down, seemingly unaffected by the hot brew.

"You seem to be enjoying your lunch," Sarah commented to Cunningham.

Niles snickered.

"These sandwiches are excellent," Cunningham said, reaching for another.

Sarah noticed that the teapot and cups were made from exquisite bone china. Nibbling on a sandwich, Sarah took a sip of tea and watched Kevin. He seemed preoccupied, as though pondering what he'd do for food and shelter when this hunting gig ran out.

"You've grown quiet, son," Cunningham commented to Kevin.

"He's been quiet all along," Niles said, "only talking when spoken to directly. Would make a fine recruit, I'd say."

"Anything on your mind?" Cunningham asked.

"Well, I was wondering what sort of animal we're after."

"Expect that you would be thinking like that," Cunningham said, taking another sandwich from the tray.

"Jolly good question," Niles added.

Cunningham took a large bite. Everyone waited patiently for him to chew, understanding that he had more to add. Holding up a finger, Cunningham signaled that it would be just another second. Then, he took a large sip of tea and looked at Kevin quizzically.

"These creatures are most unusual," Cunningham explained, "most unusual indeed."

He took another large bite of sandwich and everyone waited for him to finish chewing. Cunningham held up a finger to signal it would only be a moment, finished chewing, and then washed it down with more tea.

"As I was saying," he continued, "the creatures are like nothing we've gone after before. Never hunted anything like them, actually."

"What are they?" Sarah asked. "We've all heard about the terrible deaths, and I escaped one, but we don't know a whole lot about the creatures themselves."

"Slaughter is more like it," Niles interjected. "Tore the poor bastards to bits, pardon my language."

"As you will," Sarah said, patting down her dress.

"We are facing Rhino-pards," Cunningham explained. "They are part rhino and part leopard. Some sort of vivisection done on the Ivory Coast. A mad French scientist shacked up in a village doing unusual experiments on animals."

"A most disturbing chap," Niles added. "Most disturbing indeed. The intelligence on these creatures is alarming. The bodies are stout rhino skin and the heads are tantamount to oversized leopards, fangs—"

"With a horn jutting from the top of its nose," Cunningham interrupted. "And they're flesh-eating carnivores, with a rhino's hind legs and menacing claws on the front."

"Skin so dense the typical bullet won't penetrate it," Niles said, "which is not uncommon with some big game. They often have thick hides and solid bones, impenetrable skulls."

"Sounds quite dangerous," Sarah said, excited.

"Quite so," Cunningham responded, "quite so."

"How many are there?" Kevin said.

"We understand that there are two of them. But we've just arrived and haven't done our own investigation."

"Do you know how they got here?" Sarah asked.

"Transported over the ocean like anything else," Cunningham said. "Apparently, they were sent from *Cote de Dents* by a ship that sailed into Boston Harbor. The hoist gave way while unloading, breaking an enormous crate wide-open on the dock. The beasts scampered for shore and have been terrorizing the city ever since."

"And nobody has been connected to the receipt of this cargo," Niles added. "The bill of lading includes only an obscure limited liability company, which doesn't seem to exist."

"Why would anyone go through the trouble of shipping them here?" said Kevin.

"That's another good question, lad," Cunningham replied. "We expect the creatures were being sent into your western territories. Either to be used in some sort of zoo for a profit, or to drive out indigenous inhabitants, and claim land."

"In any event," Niles concluded, "we cannot have them roaming around Massachusetts Bay Colony."

****

They finished up the sandwiches and tea, and then Kevin sat back as Alice came to take the empty tray away. Cunningham lit up a cigar and headed to the liquor cabinet. "Would anyone care for a drink?" he said. "There appears to be a fine stock of American whiskey."

"Will do," Niles said, lighting a corncob pipe.

"My lady?" Cunningham said.

"Thank you for offering, but I'll pass."

Cunningham reached for a shiny bottle and pulled a large cork from the top, whiffed the cork, and then poured three fingers into two Old-Fashioned glasses. He spilled a couple fingers worth into a third glass.

Then, he dropped a small cube of sugar into each glass, followed by a slice of orange peel he'd commandeered from a fruit bowl. Cunningham reached for a wooden Muddler and ground the peel and cube of sugar in each glass.

Picking up two glasses, he walked over and handed one to Niles and the other to Kevin. "That will grow hair on your chest, lad."

Sarah giggled at the comment.

Kevin sniffed the whiskey, inhaling a sweet, nutty, citrus aroma. Taking a small sip, he was surprised how smooth it tasted. He had expected strong, harsh liquor. Accustomed to beer, Kevin had never tried straight whiskey, except once chugging it from a cheap bottle with a twist-off cap.

He took a bigger sip and looked over at Cunningham. The glass in the big man's hand was near empty. Niles nursed his drink, just a few sips taken, so Kevin didn't feel completely embarrassed.

"Good whiskey," Cunningham said, smiling at Kevin.

Kevin nodded in agreement.

"We'll wrap this up soon, and best get a start on earning our wages."

****

Finishing up the rest of his whiskey, Kevin stood and felt a little dizzy from the drink. He placed the glass on the tea table and stepped over to the leather portmanteau. Picking it up, he turned to Niles. "Best get cleaned up," Kevin said.

"The lavatory is down the hall under the stairs," said Niles.

"Thank you," Kevin replied, heading for the hall.

"Why in Blazes do you need a suitcase to go to a water closet?" Cunningham griped.

"Just to freshen up," Kevin offered, not even sure what was in the bag.

"Freshen up," Cunningham said, quizzically. "Like a lady powdering her nose. I thought that you were going to be our gun bearer. Toughen up!"

"Only going to wash up, brush my teeth. That sort of thing."

"Brush your teeth?" Cunningham said. "It's not even nighttime, yet."

"Ease up on the lad," Niles intervened. "He's obviously trying to clean up for the lady before we take her home."

"Right," Cunningham said, slightly chagrinned. "But toughen up anyway."

Turning down the hall, Kevin heard Sarah laugh at the bickering older men. He opened the bathroom door and used the facilities.

After washing up, Kevin opened the portmanteau on the floor. It had two separate compartments, each held shut with canvas flaps. He turned a couple of brass knobs and opened one side. Grey wool trousers and a matching suit jacket lay inside.

He turned the brass knobs of the other side and found a crisp white shirt and black tie. Something bulky lay beneath the shirt. Peeling back the garment, he expected to see a pair of dress boots or shoes.

An odd-looking weapon lay inside the suitcase, about the size of a pistol. It resembled a Ray-gun from science fiction television shows, except it was comprised of outdated parts. A polished wooden handle and forearm, the workings were brass, and the muzzle seemed to be fabricated from dark iron that flared out at the end.

Kevin inspected it carefully and sensed that it was a real weapon. He changed into the Victorian suit, and put his jackboots back on. Tucking the Ray-gun inside his wool jacket, he glanced in the mirror and noticed the weapon bulged slightly. Kevin slipped on his leather coat, further concealing the Ray-gun.

Returning, he found Niles missing from the crew. Sarah stood to leave, brushing at her dress to straighten it out. He looked at

Cunningham. High caliber rounds were stuffed in the loops above Cunningham's right breast pocket. The hunter reached for the rifle case that Kevin had carried inside, and held an even bigger case in the other hand.

"Grab that knapsack over by the dining room," Cunningham said.

Kevin saw it across the room and headed over to fetch it. "Where did Niles go?" he asked Cunningham.

"Went out to stoke the furnace of the steam Rover," Cunningham replied. "Are you all set, my lady?"

"Perfectly ready to depart," Sarah replied. "But I'd love to join you on this adventure."

"We'd very much appreciate having you along," Cunningham said. "But this is our first tracking of the creatures, and it's likely to be a bit muddy where we are headed. Perhaps another time."

"I'll take your word for it." She smiled and curtsied.

"Expect that we'll be seeing you again soon," Cunningham chuckled, and then winked at Kevin.

CHAPTER SEVEN

Outside, the temperature felt crisp as the day settled into a fall New England afternoon. Niles already had the Rover running. The furnace was stoked, and smoke emitted from the exhaust pipe protruding from the hood. Kevin and Sarah climbed into a warm vehicle and he had plenty of room without the luggage.

He focused on the task at hand, and so there wasn't much thought about his predicament. Somehow, the prospect of facing highly dangerous creatures seemed less daunting than contemplating what had happened to bring him into this strange world.

Niles backed the Rover onto the cobblestone road, and then headed uphill towards the finer neighborhoods in Boston. He sat quietly slumped behind the wheel, while Cunningham perused a map.

"Where are you hcadcd?" Sarah inquired.

"Down to Boston Harbor where it all began," Cunningham said. "We'll track this hunt from the docks and head inland."

"Wouldn't that area have already been covered?" Sarah said.

Cunningham chuckled and rubbed his walrus mustache. "Not by us, and we cannot count on the efforts of others."

"Seems slightly presumptuous," Sarah chided Cunningham. "Perhaps you've earned a reputation of being the best, and may find something they overlooked."

Niles laughed as Cunningham's face grew red with chagrin.

"I'm sure they know what they're doing," Kevin said.

"Right you are, lad," Cunningham said. "This will give us a chance to track them, confirm the size and number of the beasts. And perhaps determine where they're bedding."

"But you don't trust the judgment of others, who have already been on the scene?" Sarah asked.

"This is not a question of someone's poor judgment," Cunningham explained apologetically. "It's more a matter of *experience*."

"Do you feel that the 10th Royal Hussars are inexperienced?"

"They are a fine military outfit," Cunningham responded. "But they're not big game hunters."

Sarah nodded, conceding to Cunningham's point.

After making a few turns, the Rover splashed over muddy roads and then turned back onto a cobblestone lane. Kevin recognized the area as Louisburg Square, and Sarah had already given Niles her address.

The neighborhood was comprised of ornate Greek Revival townhouses, towering over the public street. Most were three stories tall with a fourth level for servants. The façades were clay brick. Many of the houses had a turret protruding from the living area. Windows were flanked by black shutters, and the rooftops were made of slate. Dormers jutted from the servant quarters, breaking up the roofline.

"Fine bit of architecture," Niles commented.

"Why thank you," Sarah replied. "Do you have an interest in architecture?"

"That's his bloody degree from University," Cunningham said.

"Really?"

"A member of RIBA and all," Niles explained. "But I haven't worked in the field terribly much due to military services and adventures with Silas."

"RIBA?" Sarah asked.

"Blazes, he's modest," Cunningham interjected. "Royal Institute of British Architects. Niles designed a barracks for SAS troops, and developed an addition to the Royal Palace."

"Quite impressive," Sarah said. "Quite impressive indeed."

Everyone fell quiet as the Rover cut around a square located in the middle of the posh neighborhood.

Wrought-iron fencing ran around the square: a grassy patch of land with a scattering of trees and a statue of William Pepperell, who led the fighting during the 1745 Battle of Louisburg against the French.

A few Hansom Cabs bounced over the cobblestone streets. The cabs were pulled by trotting horses that required little direction. Drivers perched themselves upon a strung-seat located behind the cab. They sat up high and drew the reins over the black, leather rooftops. The smell of manure wafted from the lane.

Niles came to a halt behind a stationary Hansom Cab. A newly acquired passenger gave the driver instructions through a trap door in the roof. Then, the cab eased into motion, with large wheels churning over the cobblestones. Each cab was fitted with brass lanterns and the spokes of the big wheels were painted a colorful yellow.

The Rover pressed ahead. "Such a lovely neighborhood," Niles said.

"A fine colony," Cunningham added, twisting the tip of his mustache.

"Thank you," Sarah replied. "I'm sure that London has its fair share of splendid neighborhoods."

"Indeed," Cunningham said. "But you won't find me living in one."

Niles snickered, but Sarah didn't quite seem to follow.

Similar wrought-iron fencing ran along the sidewalks, sealing the upper crust from pedestrian travelers. Many front doors had granite pediments, and some were flanked by cream pillars set on granite steps, descending to the sidewalks. Gardens occupied the area between the fencing and homes; small fruit trees, and an array of flowers filled the confined space. Planter's boxes hung from windows on the lower levels.

"Why this is a fine neighborhood," Cunningham repeated, cheerily. "Very fine indeed."

"Mr. Howells, the editor, lives next door," Sarah said. "And Charles Bulfinch, the architect, owns the property around the corner. My friend Louisa lived just beyond him, until they moved to a farm. When I was a little girl, I used to wish Mr. Alcott had purchased a property closer to my house, making it easier to play with Louisa. Now that she lives in the country, I'm afraid I do not see her very often."

"Appears to be a splendid place for a childhood," Niles added.

Kevin looked around and seemed to recognize the neighborhood, maybe from walking tours of Boston. In modern times, Kevin expected that Louisburg Square would be considered one of the most expensive neighborhoods in America. Listening to her description of the neighborhood, made Kevin realize that it would always be unattainable to most of society.

The Rover came to a stop and rumbled idling. Sarah remained seated in the back next to Kevin, staring ahead patiently.

Niles cleared his throat with exaggeration.

Eventually understanding that he'd held things up, Kevin climbed from the Rover and hurried to the other side of the vehicle. He opened the door and Sarah reached out with a gloved hand. Keven took hold of her hand, and then assisted her in alighting from the vehicle.

They walked up the sidewalk to her front door. Sarah turned to face Kevin. Uncertain of what to do, he froze staring at her, confused. Raising her gloved hand with a giggle, Sarah looked at Kevin flirtatiously.

He took her hand and kissed the back of it.

"My, you do catch on, Mr. Barnes."

"Shall I call on you tomorrow?"

"You may indeed," she replied. "And don't forget that I'll eventually be joining your little hunting party."

Kevin gulped nervously.

"Don't be concerned about me," Sarah said. "I'll be perfectly fine. I've faced one of those beasts before… the only person to live and talk about it."

She smiled at him and then turned to go inside.

Kevin stood on the bottom step, watching as she ascended the granite stairs, her dress flowing wide. Sarah likely sensed that he hadn't left to return to the Rover. Then, she entered a dark hallway and shut the door behind her without looking back at him, a tease.

CHAPTER EIGHT

Kevin hastily walked to the Rover. He climbed inside and met rebuke. "Blazes, lad," Cunningham snorted. "We understand she's a beauty, but we've got work to do. There's no time to stand around looking at skirts flowing upstairs."

"Didn't know we were in such a rush," Kevin said.

"Move along," Cunningham said to Niles, waving a hand. The Rover rumbled over the cobblestones. "Of course there's a rush. We can't sit around waiting for the 10th Hussars to take the beasts down. The clock is ticking, son."

Kevin didn't understand the comment. Cunningham had described the 10th Hussars as incompetent huntsmen. "But wouldn't it be a good thing…" he asked meekly, "whoever takes them down."

"My God!" Cunningham expostulated. "Whose side are you on?"

The Rover fell into silence, except for rumbling from the steam boiler. Kevin bounced occasionally from the rough cobblestone road, and each time the suspension creaked.

Niles cut around a few slow moving carts, as they traveled downhill toward the harbor.

Soon, they cleared the large city buildings and Niles accelerated the Rover. A billow of smoke shot from the exhaust pipe. They headed down Congress Street, hurrying toward the channel, separating Boston proper from a warehouse district.

The fishing peers and deep-water docks lay along Boston Harbor just beyond the shabby brick warehouses across the bridge.

As the Rover thumped across a wooden bridge, traversing the channel, Cunningham leaned over and squinted at a small monument.

"Is that what I think it is?" Cunningham said, pointing.

"A memorial of the Boston Tea Party," Kevin said.

"Blazes, why in Pete Sakes does the Empire allow this sort of dissent?"

"Just a historical marker," said Kevin.

"Anarchy, absolute anarchy," Cunningham said, pounding the dashboard. "Commemorating a day when a bunch of rabble rousers started an upheaval."

"Never seen a monument commemorating a lost war," Niles said quizzically.

Kevin slumped in his seat. All the excitement about the hunt had caused him to forget his predicament. Their comments were a reminder, not only of his situation, but of the fact that he really didn't know much about this terrene.

"Don't worry, lad," Cunningham said. "Your New Hampshire militia fared well during the war. The colonies lost mainly because of the secret treaties with France and Spain that cut off much of the supplies and support."

"Hearing that doesn't make me feel any better."

"Losing should never make you feel well," Niles commented, "especially if you're a born winner. Winners always hate to lose."

"Sounds like you're a prospect for a winner," Cunningham said. "Glad to have you along. Makes this expedition a little more interesting."

Kevin thought Cunningham actually sounded sincere.

They rambled over the end of the bridge and cruised past a few warehouses. Following the brick buildings, a street wound to the right, lined in triple-decker, multifamily houses, with clapboard siding. Each level had a porch overlooking the street. Past the houses lay a flat plain of land, covered in tall grass, which dropped off at the ragged coastline.

Beyond the grassy plain, lay wharves, and then the choppy waters of Boston Harbor. The scene depicted a port city hard at work. A few fishing piers jutted from the coastline on the left. Boats plodded along trying to make their daily catch. On the right stood a few deep-water docks.

Vast wooden sailing ships were tied at the docks, thick ropes fastened to the piles; steam cranes worked hard unloading the cargo. Wagons pulled by dray horses hauled freight off the big docks, plank beds sagging under the weight of heavy loads.

Upon the water, an immense schooner was being escorted to a dock, sails rolled up. Little steam tug boats nosed the schooner along, spitting black smoke from stacks protruding from the pilot cabins.

An ominous dark boat patrolled the harbor. Cannon ports were located along the iron-plated sides just above the waterline; most of the hull was submerged in the murky water. Smoke billowed from twin stacks jutting from the flat roof, and a Union Jack fluttered at the stern. The city-class ironclad gunboat seemed to be roving the harbor in methodical, constant motion.

Niles maneuvered the Rover toward the deep-water dock that moored two ships. They parked on the edge of the thick grass and climbed out.

"We'll leave the rifles here for now," Cunningham said, walking hastily toward the dock. "But grab that knapsack, lad. Might need what's in there."

Kevin slipped the knapsack over a shoulder and headed after them. Cunningham rushed toward the dock and Niles hustled to keep up. The hunters pulled further ahead as Kevin struggled to catch them.

Cunningham stood on the edge of the dock, feet planted shoulder-width apart, with Niles beside him. The Great Hunter reached for his breast pocket and pulled out a piece of paper. Kevin approached and realized Cunningham held a rough sketch.

Peering over a shoulder, Kevin noticed the sketch depicted a ship that likely transported the beasts. A steam crane had been staged on the dock. The drawing had a rectangle where the crate had crashed.

"Wonder if that's the steam crane in question," Cunningham said, pointing to a crane unloading a nearby ship.

"Suppose it could be our crane," Niles responded, "or one very much like it."

Instead of inspecting the spot where the wooden cargo container had broken open, Cunningham stepped to the location of the steam crane on his drawing. He carefully spied the crane working to unload the nearby ship, taking in the actions of the operator, and then turned and began to act out the unloading of the Rhino-pards.

"The report indicated that the hoist gave way," Niles said. "So, this exercise could prove to be a waste of time."

"Rubbish," Cunningham retorted. His hands worked make-believe levers, as he intently scanned the scene.

Niles watched Cunningham curiously. "You think something else happened?"

"Look at that piling to the left," Cunningham said.

Kevin and Niles turned to view the piling. It had a sizable gash in the side where something had swung into it and splintered the wood.

"That could have happened any time in recent months," Niles finally responded.

"But look over here," Cunningham said, pointing at the dock near his imaginary cockpit. "See where the dock is chewed up. That's from the crane tipping."

"Looks fairly recent."

"The operator got distracted by something over there," Cunningham explained. "He swung the beam too far, causing the crane to tip. The crate swung wide and crashed into the piling."

"Then the Rhino-pards burst through the broken crate."

"Right you are, Niles," said Cunningham. "After hitting the piling, the crane would have righted itself, causing the crate to swing back."

Kevin noticed claw marks in the dock. "And they jumped out right here," he said, indicating to striations in the wood.

Cunningham smiled proudly.

"Right you are, lad," Cunningham said.

"They broke free and trampled along the edge of the dock," Niles said, walking toward shore.

Kevin and Cunningham followed after Niles. There were sporadic claw marks in the dock as the Rhino-pards tore off, fleeing the pier. Glancing at the claw marks, Kevin estimated the width at sixteen centimeters.

There were also a number of gnarled planks along the edge of the dock, aligning with some claw marks. Bits of wood were churned up from the pounding beasts.

Cunningham waved for them to halt at the end of the dock. He looked around and then pointed to a Rhino-pard print in the muddy shoreline to the right. There were a few more prints beyond it.

Leading the way, Cunningham slowly stepped along the shore, being careful to walk to the side of the tracks. Kevin and Niles trailed a meter behind. The tracks snaked along the tideline.

"Blazes!" Cunningham said, halting. "Would you look at that?"

A number of boot prints intermingled with the tracks in the mud.

"Bloody shameful," he added, shaking his head.

Approaching another dock, the tracks veered away from the water and disappeared into tall grass. A multitude of boot prints jumbled throughout the mud near the point where the Rhino-pards entered the brush.

"This is where the trail ended for our predecessors," Cunningham jeered.

"What do we do from here?" Kevin whispered to Niles.

"Wait for him to figure it out."

Cunningham bent down on one knee and tilted his head low to the brush. Then he stood and walked a few paces along the shore and did it again. Wind blew off the water; he got up and took a deep breath while scanning the coastline.

There was a slope from the shoreline to the grassy plain. Many locations had steep grassy embankments stemming three meters high.

"How big are these creatures?" he said to Niles.

"From the size of the paws and back feet," Niles responded, "I'd say they approximate a small, younger rhino."

"Not a full-sized adult?"

"Heavens no."

"More like a White Rhino than a Great Horned Rhino?"

"Correct," Niles answered. "These are likely 1.5 meters high, and weigh closer to a ton, slightly over that."

"Not the two-thousand pounders that we hunted in India?"

"These are smaller," Niles agreed. "But they appear to be much more agile."

Cunningham nodded, seeming to understand, and then he examined the grassy embankment further. Suddenly, he turned and inspected the muddy shore, squinting and running a hand over his pate.

He walked off without saying a word, trailing the edge of the grass where it meets shore. Mud clumped to the soles of Cunningham's boots as he plodded along. Eventually, he bent down and stared at a rivulet trickling from the grass. A tiny stream of water meandered into the harbor.

Then, Cunningham stood erect and turned toward the grassy embankment. Hands on hips, he spied the grass for a moment, staring at the hillside, and then he scanned along the grassy plain.

"And they're certainly smarter than your typical rhino," he finally said.

"How so?" Niles said.

Cunningham pointed at a spot in the embankment where the grass stood tall and thick. "Right there," he said.

Nothing appeared visible except tall brush.

"What do you have there, chap?" Niles inquired.

Tracing with a finger, Cunningham indicated from the embankment back toward where the muddy boot prints were located. He intimated as though this explained everything. It didn't enlighten Kevin as to what the Great Hunter had fixated upon.

Niles looked confused as well.

Breaking from the shoreline, Cunningham plied his way through the tall grass. "This way, my lads," he commanded.

****

Following Niles through the tall grass, Kevin reached the embankment long after Cunningham. They found him looking things over peculiarly. He peeked around the brush scratching his head.

"What is it?" Niles said.

"Should have brought a machete," Cunningham said.

"Didn't think we'd need one in the city," Niles said. "After all, it's not like we're in the African bush."

"Stand back," Cunningham instructed, and then he whacked at the brush with his hand. Crabgrass flew in sundry directions until the mouth of a large steel pipe was revealed. Kevin lent a hand and uprooted more brush.

The steel pipe was three meters in diameter. A steady trickle of water dripped from the end of the pipe, meandering through reeds and crabgrass toward the shore.

"They plunged through the brush into the pipe," Cunningham explained. "Did it so quickly that the grass popped back into place."

"So that's how they disappeared from view," Niles reasoned. "And no one could track them from there."

"With all the commotion on the dock," Cunningham said, "nobody even saw them dive in here."

"How could the Rhino-pards have known?" Kevin asked.

"Definitely very smart," Niles said. "Very bright indeed."

"Probably sensed the water and jumped through here," Cunningham said. "Like plowing past a waterfall into a hidden cave."

Something caught Cunningham's attention. He reached for a piece of material stuck on the side of the shiny metal pipe. Kevin couldn't make out the object. It seemed like a scrap of rubber tire, like retread torn loose on the open highway.

Cunningham turned and held it up.

"They busted through here so fast and hard," he said, "that one of them caught its hide on the pipe there."

Niles looked it over. "These things have skin like the armor-plated tanks that we used in the Great War."

Cunningham nodded in agreement.

They stood there looking at the pipe for a moment. A glimmer of daylight shone inside for about three to four meters, and then the pipe extended into extreme darkness. The total length of the pipe was difficult to determine.

"What in blazes is this pipe used for?" Cunningham expostulated.

Niles climbed up the embankment and looked around. He quickly honed in on something and so Kevin and Cunningham trudged up the hillside. A large factory building jutted in the distance, constructed from brick. Five enormous smoke stacks towered from the back of the building.

"A cogeneration facility," Niles said.

"Why the pipe?" Cunningham asked.

"The facility is a power plant for combined electric and heat," Niles explained. "The city is likely getting power and heat for its various public buildings from that facility. Steam is the source of heat and power. The perfect location for such a facility, actually."

"You still haven't explained the pipe."

"They take water from the ocean, purify it, and then use coal to heat it into steam," Niles continued. "The steam creates energy that they conduct through lines running underground. The same tunnels carry typical steam pipes for heating buildings."

"So this pipe is just a conduit for electrical lines and steam pipes?" Cunningham questioned. "But why doesn't anything come out on this end?"

"A future line?" Kevin guessed.

"Heavens no," Niles answered. "This here is a major condensate line for the facility. You see, all steam lines carry steam along the top of the pipe, which is used for heating and gets into radiators in buildings. But a natural by-product of steam is condensate, water. If not drained from the line, the condensate can affect the system. It naturally travels across the bottom of the piping and drains out at low points, through drainpipes and drip-legs."

"So, this pipe drains all the condensate from the system?" Cunningham said.

"Not quite," Niles answered. "This is likely a major drainpipe for the boiler and other drain lines may run into it. There are underground vaults all around the city where piping enters and exits. The pipes entering the vaults deposit the condensate into the vaults by exiting drip-legs."

"What are the drip-legs?" Kevin said.

"Just smaller pipes attached to the bottom of the steam lines," Niles said. "Valves can be opened or closed to allow for drainage into the drip-legs."

"So the drip-legs are attached to the bottom of a big steam pipe. And the condensate runs along the bottom of the pipe and drains out the drip-legs."

"That's about right, lad," Niles confirmed. "But only when the valves are open. The drip-legs are usually smaller pipes than the steam lines they are attached to."

Kevin nodded understanding.

"And so that is why steam lines are tapped on top of the line," Niles said, "when diverting steam in different directions."

"To allow the steam to continue upward and along the pipe, while the condensate runs along the bottom and drips out?" Kevin asked.

"Correct."

"There were attacks in various parts of the city," Cunningham said. "If this pipe merely runs back to that factory, how do you explain it?"

"Maybe it connects with another pipe, or a tunnel," Niles answered. "Or perhaps they came back out."

Cunningham stood there contemplating.

"So what's next?" Niles asked.

"Get the rifles, lad!" Cunningham commanded. "We've got ourselves a hunt."

CHAPTER NINE

Kevin dashed over bent grass heading to the Rover. His boots sunk into the mud that oozed between fallen reeds. Reaching the edge of matted crabgrass, he took a deep breath. Malodorous saltwater and low-tide muck pierced his nostrils.

He hurried along the shoreline as the ironclad chugged through choppy water twenty meters offshore. An extraordinary show of power. Waves broke against its bow, splashing onto the low decking, and smoke rhythmically spit from twin stacks protruding from the ship.

A stern sailor leaned near an open canon hatch. His face looked gaunt and hard, smeared in soot. He seemed impervious to the damp, chilly sea breeze. Although the sailor appeared haggard, Kevin suspected they were a similar age.

Cunningham jolted Kevin from thoughtful contemplation. "Get moving, lad!" he yelled. "And bring the Gibbs."

Double-timing back to the Rover, Kevin glanced back and caught Cunningham grinning. Then, the Great Hunter slapped Niles on the shoulder, seeming excited the hunt was finally underway.

Kevin jogged by the end of the deep-water dock. A couple of workers jeered at him, motioning to the tops of their heads. They obviously found his purple Mohawk funny. He didn't pay them any mind and headed straight for the Rover.

Parked on a knoll above the embankment, the Rover was surrounded by tall grass. The big tires pressed the reeds down, but the rest of the crabgrass had sprung back up. Kevin forged his way through waist-high grass and opened a rear door. Reaching for the Gibbs, he thought over Cunningham's instructions.

Initially, they told him to get the rifles, then Cunningham demanded the Gibbs. It wasn't clear if Cunningham wanted all of the rifles, or only the Gibbs. Slinging the Gibbs .505 over a shoulder with the barrel pointed down, Kevin thought about the weapon that Cunningham had used in Canada. Kevin reached for the Weatherby .460 elephant gun.

After deciding upon the Weatherby and the Gibbs, Kevin grabbed two ammunition belts, each full of rounds for the respective rifles. He slung the belts across his chest, and then slipped the Weatherby onto the free shoulder.

Kevin steadily marched back to the oversized pipe, grasping the slings of both rifles to steady the weapons. Dense stocks jabbed into his shoulders, and the rifles weighed him down. By the time he returned, Kevin's legs had begun to tire and his shoulders were chafed from the slings.

Niles had the knapsack on his back and a kerosene lantern by his side.

Standing nearby, Cunningham wore his Australian bush hat, while peeking into the pipe. He wore a pistol in a leather holster slung through a web belt with a brass buckle. The holster had a flap with the stamp of the crown, concealing the butt of the pistol. Cunningham seemed to notice Kevin, and walked over; he reached for the Weatherby.

Niles took hold of the Gibbs. Kevin felt glad to be rid of the burdensome load, and relieved that he'd brought the correct rifles. Both hunters removed the caps off of the scopes and put them in the knapsack, then they checked the rifles over, working the bolts.

They loaded each rifle with ammunition, making sure to chamber a round. Cunningham clicked the safety on and handed the Weatherby back to Kevin.

"Don't you want the rifle?" Kevin asked.

"We hired you to be a gun bearer," Cunningham responded. "Toughen up, and carry the rifles. We'll let you know when we need them."

Niles finished checking over the Gibbs, flicked on the safety, and then handed it to Kevin.

Taking the rifle, Kevin slung it over his left shoulder, barrel pointed down. He eased the Weatherby onto the right shoulder and grabbed the slings.

****

They started into the tunnel with Niles in the lead holding the lantern. Cunningham followed Niles. And Kevin plugged along bent slightly forward, holding the slings tightly. The daylight at the entrance of the pipe only provided illumination for ten meters. After that, each step led them farther and farther into blackness.

The lantern only shed enough light for Niles to lead the way. Trailing behind Cunningham's bulk, Kevin sloshed through the wet pipe in the shadow of the Great Hunter. He could barely perceive the clumps of debris scattered throughout the tunnel: twigs, moss, and mounds of silt. Detritus had entered the pipe and flown along the rivulet until snagging.

Shimmers of light guided Kevin's way. Occasionally, he tripped or stumbled on debris, indiscernible in the shadows. He worried about falling, and scraping a rifle on the pipe.

Both rifles were pristine with shiny stocks and impeccable barrels. Not like his Winchester .30-30 lever action. A nicked stock, the Winchester had worn bluing on the muzzle, where rain cascaded off the roof of his deer stand. He'd built the deer stand in a pine tree with his father near their hunting lodge in Maine. After a few rainy hunting seasons, the two got the idea to build an overhang. They caught some flak from guys at the camp, but always came back drier than the rest of them.

Occasionally, after Kevin stumbled, Cunningham snapped at him to be careful. Kevin wanted to explain the poor light, but he knew Cunningham wouldn't accept any excuses. He'd just tell Kevin to toughen up.

The pipe eventually leveled off, so less debris appeared underfoot. Sloshing along, Kevin felt water inside his jackboots. The mud and water streaming through the pipe soaked his boots, turning both socks soggy. He hadn't expected to carry the rifles the entire way. Kevin's calf muscles tightened from the extra load and waterlogged boots.

There wasn't any indication that Cunningham would stop and take a break. The pipe seemed to extend forever into darkness. At first, Kevin could see daylight pouring from the mouth of the pipe. After a series of subtle turns, daylight slipped from view. Underground in the middle of nowhere, they slogged through a pipe in utter blackness, except for scant light emanating from the lantern.

Kevin felt claustrophobic. The top of the pipe was merely centimeters over their heads, low enough that Niles had to stoop. Cunningham didn't pay the conditions any mind; he barreled along, unconcerned with discomfort or fear.

The thought of earth above them, pressing down on the pipe, daunted Kevin. He hoped for rest, but part of him just wanted to get it done, as quickly as possible. He distracted himself by focusing on other things. And then his thoughts eventually turned to the Rhino-pards.

"What if the beasts are up ahead?" he said.

"We'd certainly hear them," Cunningham replied. "And blazes, the sound you're making... splashing through the water... would certainly scare away the most ferocious beast in the jungle."

Niles chuckled.

"What if they're attracted to the light?"

"We'd shoot them, of course," Cunningham said. "That's the job that we're getting paid to do."

"Relax, lad," Niles assured him. "They've gotten to the surface and killed a few people, so the Rhino-pards have likely moved well beyond here."

"They're bedding somewhere under the city," Cunningham added, "not too far from our flat, judging from the where the attacks have occurred."

"But most big game roam a large territory, right?"

Niles smirked and patted the Great Hunter on the shoulder. "Sounds like you've got an upcoming big game hunter on your hands," he said to Cunningham.

"Seems to have some knowledge," Cunningham agreed.

The three of them continued on in silence, drudging through the dank tunnel. The lantern swung back and forth slightly, occasionally cascading shimmers of light upon the sides of the pipe.

Niles halted abruptly.

Cunningham stopped as well, his bulk obscuring the view ahead. There was no way for Kevin to see why the hunters had come to a standstill. A second passed into two, but Kevin was afraid to break the silence and ask why they stopped.

Then, Niles sloshed over to the side of the pipe, the lantern swinging widely as he stepped away. Peering around Cunningham, a pipe intersected with the one they were traveling through. The Great Hunter stepped alongside Niles and looked it over.

"What do you make of it?" Cunningham asked.

A large corrugated metal hatch stood alongside the opening. The hatch was housed in a track, so it could slide shut, blocking off the intersecting tunnel.

"Makes a lot of sense," Niles replied.

"How so?"

"The condensate drain pipe only needed to be a meter wide by my rough estimation," Niles answered. "This intersecting pipe is likely connected to the tunnel system under the city."

"For draining excess storm-water from the sewer system?" Kevin suggested.

"Exactly," Niles said. "During heavy storms, the sewers get overwhelmed and would back up into the street, unless the water had a place to drain."

"So they connected a sewer overflow pipe to the condensate line," Kevin said. "And they installed this hatch to allow the overflow line to drain through the condensate line when needed."

"That's correct," Niles confirmed, holding the lantern closer to the hatch. "You can see from the rusty tracks that they just keep it open all the time. Try giving it a shove."

Kevin walked over and grabbed the side of the hatch. It had jagged edges, so he carefully grabbed hold of it, and then he lunged forward pushing with his body weight. The hatch didn't budge.

"The Rhino-pards likely went this way," Niles said, pointing to the intersecting pipe.

"This would explain how they surfaced in the city," Cunningham said.

"We've come quite a distance," Niles said. "This pipe is likely to lead under the channel fairly soon."

"Shouldn't we let someone know that we're down here?" Kevin said.

"Why the blazes would we need to do that?" Cunningham quipped.

"What if someone closes the hatch and we're trapped down here?" Kevin said. "Or water could release from a tank and flood the system."

"Son, you have quite an imagination."

"The hatch is all but rusted permanently open," Niles said. "But he could have a point about a cistern releasing water somewhere ahead."

"Toughen up, both of you," Cunningham snapped. "There's no time for doubling back. The 10th Hussars have a head start on us, and we need to press on."

Neither of them responded to Cunningham. Instead, Niles took the lead and headed down the side tunnel, and Kevin plodded along after them.

CHAPTER TEN

Later, Niles remained in the lead with Cunningham a step or two behind him. Although a similar pipe, it wasn't as wide as the prior tunnel. The pipe seemed tighter, causing Kevin to trail further in the rear, so he couldn't see much ahead.

They plugged along without talking, and the temperature grew colder. Kevin noticed moist clouds puffing from his face. He buttoned his wool jacket, but it did little to ward off the dampness.

Niles stopped. He reached out and touched the side of the pipe.

"We're under the channel," he said.

Kevin felt condensation on the cold, steel pipe. He thought about the seawater above them and suddenly felt claustrophobic. The lantern cast light upon the ceiling of the tunnel. He noticed seams in the pipe every six meters. The seams were from sections of piping welded together to form a long drain line. Water dripped from the seams. Merely condensation, but he gulped, wondering just how much saturated earth separated the pipe from the floor of the channel.

They slugged further through the pipe. Kevin breathed hard; his legs grew weary from the excursion. Niles stepped forward and suddenly dropped down a foot. A loud splash, and the lantern wavered.

Light cast upon the walls shimmered about, revealing aged brick. Cunningham froze. Niles teetered forward. For a moment, it seemed like Niles would crash into an older tunnel wall. He grasped wires running along the side of the old tunnel and steadied himself.

"Blazes, are you all right, man?" said Cunningham.

"Watch your step," Niles responded. "Almost lost it there."

The lantern flickered. Niles stood knee-deep in murky water; he held the lantern as they looked around. The steel pipe came to an abrupt end and then picked up with a brick tunnel. The flooring of the old tunnel rest only a foot below the bottom of the pipe.

"What a nasty tunnel," Cunningham said.

"Most dreadful," Niles agreed. "This water is knee-high and likely pestiferous."

"Nothing like Calcutta," Cunningham boasted. "We'll be just fine."

After the lantern settled, the view of the tunnel became clearer. Brick catacombs lay ahead. The wires Niles held didn't run into the steel pipe. Another brick passageway led off to the side and the wires followed it.

"Which way do you want to go?" Niles asked Cunningham.

Cunningham stroked his chin and squinted down both tunnels. "Straight ahead," he said. "The beasts were likely moving at a good clip, and wouldn't have made an abrupt right angle turn."

"Good thinking," Niles said. "The Great Tracker."

"Great Hunter," Cunningham corrected. "Despise the term 'tracker' that some colonists use to describe our work. Let's move along now."

Then, Cunningham stepped into the brick tunnel, plunging into the water. He sunk enough that the Australian safari hat dropped below the height of Kevin's chest. Even being aware of the drop, Cunningham seemed surprised by the extent of the murky decent, wobbling slightly.

Filthy water rippled around Cunningham's knees. The Great Hunter and Niles stood submerged in the water. The rifle barrels would sink below the surface if Kevin stepped off the edge.

"When I step down," Kevin said, "the rifles are going to plunge into the water."

"Blazes, we can't have that happen."

"What do you want to do about it?" Niles said.

"Hand the Weatherby to me," Cunningham instructed, turning toward Kevin with his hands reaching out.

Kevin slipped the rifle from his shoulder and handed it to Cunningham.

"Hand the other one to Niles," Cunningham said.

Niles took the Gibbs. Relieved of the burden, Kevin took a deep breath and prepared to descend into the brick tunnel. He looked at the squalid water and reluctantly stepped down, submerging more than he had expected, despite watching Niles and Cunningham.

As he sunk into the water, Kevin lost balance and tilted forward. He extended an arm and braced himself on Cunningham's girth. This enabled Kevin to quickly right himself.

"Watch it there, lad," Cunningham said. "You might push me over and get the Weatherby wet."

"Whatever you do," Niles lectured, "don't mess up the Weatherby."

"Cares more about that rifle than himself," Kevin said. "The water is likely contaminated, too."

"You've got it right," Niles chuckled.

"Ready to move along?" Cunningham interjected.

"All set now," Kevin said.

"Enough chatting," Cunningham snapped. "Let's move along then."

Niles handed the rifle back to Kevin. He obviously noted the surprised look on Kevin's face. "Well, you can't expect me to carry the lantern and the rifle."

"You're a gun bearer," Cunningham snapped. "Bear the bloody rifle."

Plying their way through the knee-deep water, the pace was even slower than before. Kevin's arms tired quickly from toting the Gibbs. Stepping through the squalid water was like walking in cement shoes. Kevin felt as though he'd traded the burden of lugging two rifles for a different hardship, which drained his stamina and wearied his legs.

This passageway seemed to be antiquated, constructed of old-fashioned clay bricks and thick mortar that cured ages ago. Kevin wondered if moisture had begun to weaken the cement. A wall could cave in or the roof might collapse. Scraping the ceiling with a fingernail, the mortar felt coarse and hard. He inspected the walls and got the same result.

Fear of a collapse slipped away. Sloshing through the water caused Kevin's mind to wander. His thoughts turned to dysentery from breathing the moist air. He also suspected that sewage mixed into the storm-water overflow during severe weather.

They plugged along for a bit, making dismal progress, but pressed steadily ahead. Moving in silence, the thought of rats began to consume Kevin. He pushed the fear away, thinking that Niles and Cunningham would encounter them first. Worse than a concern over rats, he had an underlying fear of the Rhino-pards. They could lunge from a side passageway before being detected, wreaking havoc without time to react. He could still get mauled.

Kevin found himself thinking *'toughen up'* to help squelch his fears. The depth of the water eventually lessened, and they began to push ahead faster. Cunningham and Kevin held the rifles at port arms to avoid getting them wet. Making good progress, Kevin focused on his footing and keeping pace. Then Niles came to a halt.

Peering between the hunters, Kevin noticed a fork in the tunnels.

"Which way do you want to go?" Niles said.

"The one to the left," Cunningham replied without hesitation.

"You can't seriously think that we have a chance of accurately tracking them now."

"Indeed, I do," Cunningham scoffed. "To the left, man."

Niles glanced at both passageways. He shook his head. Neither was discernible from the other, and Kevin suspected that Niles thought the same.

"Suit yourself," Niles said, heading down the tunnel to the left.

The lantern swung from his abrupt turn into the dark passage. It seemed even blacker than before. Nowhere along their sojourn had any daylight entered the tunnels. Kevin noticed that the dark brick walls didn't reflect light as the metal pipe had done previously.

Further away from the fork, the water level decreased until it was ankle high. Cunningham turned and handed the Weatherby to Kevin.

"Shoulder the rifles, lad."

"Sure thing."

Kevin slung each rifle over a shoulder with the barrels facing down. By the time he finished harnessing his load, the hunters were well ahead of him.

He sloshed along in haste, leaning forward with his thumbs looped around the slings to steady the rifles. As Kevin closed the distance, Niles stopped unexpectedly. Cunningham collided into him. The lantern swung back and forth.

And then Kevin plowed into Cunningham.

The two hunters stood frozen and mute. Cunningham didn't quip about Kevin bumping into him. Another moment and they still didn't move. Standing there piled on top of each other, Kevin didn't dare move either.

Cunningham's broad shoulders and wide-brimmed hat prevented Kevin from peeking over them. He couldn't discern why they'd stopped.

The silence made him think that a passage or hatch lay ahead.

A mild thrashing in the water a meter in front of Niles changed his mind. There was something down here with them.

Kevin snooped under Cunningham's elbow, expecting to see rats.

There was a shredded torso strewn in the putrid water. A saturated lavender dress with a ruffled collar torn to bits, splattered in blood. The extremities were severed in rough, jagged tears. Meat was cleaved from the bone. Even the head was missing.

An immense claw pressed the torso into the floor of the tunnel, protectively. Water bubbled up around the paw. Kevin felt a shiver run down his spine. Two large golden cat eyes shimmered at them from the darkness. The outline of a large leopard head shone in the refracting glow of the lantern. A dense horn protruded from its snout.

Its thick neck tapered out to the colossal body of a rhinoceros. Protective skin covered the massive beast resembling menacing armor-plating. The skin folded at the joints of muscular hind legs and shoulders.

The tracking team remained frozen in silence. Waiting for the beast to make a move, the hunters stood a meter away, vulnerable. Yellow eyes fixated upon them, stern and intelligent, never wavering in the lamplight.

Thrashing in the water behind the beast caused it to look away. The other Rhino-pard had come up behind it.

"Rifle," Cunningham whispered.

Kevin slowly slipped the Weatherby from his shoulder.

Sensing movement in the tunnel, the beast turned back to them. Cunningham had the rifle at port arms but hesitated shouldering it.

The beast stomped on the bloody torso, shook its head ferociously, and then bared huge fangs, dripping with saliva. Fur around its mouth was smeared crimson from feasting upon the dead woman.

Behind the beast, the other Rhino-pard seemed agitated, slamming into the tunnel walls. A few bricks popped loose, and the two immense creatures bucked into each other. Kevin feared they would stampede through the tunnel, crushing the entire tracking team.

Turning its head, the beast let out a deep cat-like hiss at its companion. Cunningham worked the bolt. A metallic echo rang through the tunnel. The creature snapped back to them, eyeing the tracking party suspiciously. Cunningham raised the rifle. The Rhino-pard sniffed the dank air, and then snatched up the torso in its teeth and wheeled around in the narrow tunnel. The beasts' shoulders and haunches pounded into the brick walls.

Both Rhino-pards quickly changed direction. Mortar in the tunnel walls cracked and bricks splashed into the water. Then, the creatures charged off, tearing down the passageway.

A few irate growls emanated over the heavy stomping, which splashed through the water as the Rhino-pards pounded away.

Cunningham lowered the rifle and shook his head.

Niles turned to the Great Hunter, beads of sweat dripping from his brow. "That was close," Niles said.

"Too close to shoot," Cunningham said, "unless absolutely necessary."

Niles nodded.

"When an animal is that close," Cunningham explained to Kevin, "it can take a hit and still maul you to death."

"By the way," Niles interrupted. "Did you see the density of its hide?"

"Never seen such a thick protective hide."

"Me either."

"Not on a rhino, hippo, or even an elephant."

"Do you expect that it's part of the vivisection?"

"Makes me wonder what we're dealing with," Cunningham responded. "Neither a leopard, nor a rhino has a hide that thick. And mixing the two creatures shouldn't result in an attribute more perfected than on one of them alone."

"Except where the mix causes an enhancement."

"Right," Cunningham agreed. "Take the fangs for instance. They're an attribute of the leopard and rhino, so the mix makes them larger. But this issue with the hide—"

"Seems like the creatures are scientifically enhanced," Niles cut in. "And not just a blend of two species."

"Absolutely."

"They're really smart, too," Kevin added, meekly.

The two hunters paused and turned toward Kevin.

"That's a good observation," Cunningham said. "A good observation indeed."

"These aren't ordinary creatures," Niles added. "They appear to be very intelligent for big game. And they're highly adaptable."

Cunningham nodded.

"They quickly made use of this tunnel system," Niles said. "The change in climate doesn't seem to have fazed them either."

"And they're hell-bent on survival," Cunningham concluded. "Pardon my language, but it's true."

"Appears to be the case," Niles said. "The beasts have cognitive ability, adaptability, and I dare say, a certain amount of experience that is retained."

"Certainly understood the Weatherby," Cunningham chuckled.

"Indeed. Although I'm not certain that I sensed an extreme fear."

"Didn't seem like fear at all," Cunningham said. "More like a decision to take their spoils and be off with it."

"Makes sense. If they had encountered rifles in the past," Niles reasoned, "it wasn't severe enough to inflict a mortal wound. Otherwise, they wouldn't be here."

Cunningham left the round chambered, flicked on the safety, and then slung the rifle over his shoulder. The tracking party was not about to disband. Then, Niles held a hand out toward Kevin.

Handing over the Gibbs, Kevin felt vulnerable. Beforehand, he would have been happy to be released of the burden. After seeing the Rhino-pards, he felt more comfortable holding a rifle.

"Lead on," Cunningham said to Niles.

"Guess you were right back there at the fork."

"Apparently so," Cunningham said, laughing.

The break was brief, with just enough time to catch their breath and fairly little discussion. Kevin wondered how the two of them could function so well without much verbal communication.

CHAPTER ELEVEN

Proceeding down the tunnel single file, Niles took the lead again, holding onto the lantern. He had the Gibbs slung over his left shoulder, clinging to the leather sling with a free hand.

Cunningham walked three paces back, carrying the Weatherby at port arms. He was ready to raise the rifle and fire past Niles at a moment's notice. Trailing behind them, Kevin didn't carry anything, and had an even harder time seeing ahead, now that the column was spread out.

The two hunters plodded along sloshing through ankle-high water. Comforted by the rifles, the hunters didn't reveal any sign of fear. Kevin was terrified of the Rhino-pards. He'd heard stories of high caliber bullets getting lodged in the jaw bones of grizzly bears. He wondered if the Rhino-pards' dense hides and thick bones would prevent the elephant guns from taking them down.

Kevin patted his wool jacket and felt the Ray-gun. Having it along didn't assuage his concerns. He wasn't even sure how to use the avant-garde weapon. And his fear began to escalate, wondering if the beasts might circle around and approach from the rear. They had encountered enough side passageways. Surely, the catacombs under the city tied together, and the Rhino-pards had learned their way through the maze.

Eventually, the tunnel leveled off so the water only rose above the soles of their boots. Now, light bulbs in protective cages hung overhead, and the brick walls appeared more soiled. A patch of soot rubbed onto the elbow of Cunningham's safari coat.

They slogged along a little further and came upon a metal ladder affixed to the wall; it clearly ascended to the street above.

"Appears to be a manhole access," Niles said.

"We're under the city for sure," Cunningham said. "Let's press on a little further. Then we'll go topside."

"The manhole covers are likely secured," Niles remarked.

"The Rhino-pards have a way out," Cunningham said. "Blazes, we'll find a means out of the tunnel as well."

"Could take longer to find it," Niles considered, "than to double back, though."

Kevin's stomach dropped at the thought of heading back the way they had come, but Cunningham didn't respond to the suggestion. He just chuckled knowingly and continued to slosh ahead.

They came upon a few side passages and more ladders leading to manholes on the surface. Daylight seeped through gaps around the manhole covers. Kevin grew more comfortable at the sight of light. He figured they would find a means of egress now that they were under the city.

Most of the side passages were lone tunnels venturing off the main passageway. The crew eventually came upon a four-way intersection. Cunningham slung the Weatherby over his shoulder.

Niles stopped and handed the lantern to Cunningham instinctively. Kevin noticed the two had worked together for so long that they sometimes did things without speaking. The Great Hunter quietly studied the intersecting tunnels. He paid particular attention to the edges of each tunnel entrance. Holding the lantern and bending over, Cunningham inspected the sides to each of the passageways.

He picked at the brick with a fingernail, and then reached for the large hunting knife sheathed on his web belt. Cunningham pried something loose and handed it to Niles. It looked like another scrap of Rhino-pard hide, similar to what had torn loose on the metal pipe opening by the shoreline.

After that, Cunningham looked at the ceiling and the walls; he seemed content with his inspection. Cunningham carved an "X" into the brick with the tip of his knife, then stepped over to Niles.

Niles took the lantern. "What do you think?" he asked Cunningham.

"This is a cross-passageway," Cunningham said, studying the wall. "They seem to use it for getting from a nesting location to an access point topside."

Niles nodded in agreement, and then Cunningham stepped ahead. He began marching down the tunnel to the right.

"Hurry it up now," Cunningham barked. "We haven't got all day."

Niles picked up his pace and caught up to Cunningham. The tunnel had a slight upgrade and soon they were walking upon dry concrete. Cunningham and Niles pressed forward moving down the tunnel fairly carefree, as though neither of them anticipated running into the Rhino-pards again. Kevin rushed along behind them trying to keep up. Still afraid.

They followed the tunnel for some time until Cunningham came to an abrupt halt. He took out his knife and carved another "X" into the brick. Through the darkness, Kevin noticed a smaller passageway to the left.

Cunningham pointed at the narrow tunnel, directing Niles to approach it. They inspected the edges of the small passageway. More scraps of protective skin had torn off on the brick.

He handed the Weatherby to Kevin and then sauntered down the narrow passage behind Niles. The tunnel took a slight turn. Kevin could sense their path bending to the right. When the tunnel straightened out, pockets of light broke through the darkness ahead of them.

So much daylight was uplifting, but Kevin couldn't discern why the patch of light was distorted. He estimated the end of the tunnel at about thirty meters. The brighter the tunnel got, the more Cunningham picked up his pace, pulling ahead of Niles.

As they moved closer to the end of the tunnel, Kevin's eyes were blinded by the brightness. They were almost at the end when Kevin realized that a wall of greenery covered the tunnel opening. Then he noticed iron grating and his hope dissipated.

He dreaded the thought of turning back. Then, he noticed Cunningham inspecting the grate curiously. The big game hunter grabbed an iron bar and gave it a shake. The metal rattled in his hand, but held firm.

"Come on, fellas," he said, "this way."

Cunningham stepped to the side of the tunnel and gave the grating a good shove. It wobbled loose, leaving a gap about a meter wide. He squeezed through the aperture and then scrambled into thick brush.

Niles cut off the lantern and followed after Cunningham. Although Kevin loathed the idea of scraping through bushes, he would brave almost anything to flee the dank tunnel. He slipped past the grate, carefully trying to avoid damaging the Weatherby. Then, he worked his way through the brush, slowly easing around the branches. Kevin tried to follow the path that Cunningham had taken, but still got jabbed by an occasional sharp branch.

Once he cleared the dense bushes, Kevin found Cunningham and Niles standing on a grassy hillside. He looked around and realized the opening led into the common they'd passed on the way to Cunningham's quarters.

CHAPTER TWELVE

Standing on the hillside, Cunningham cleared the chambers of both rifles, and then handed them to Kevin. They seemed to weigh even more than before, and the slings immediately ached his chafed shoulders.

The Great Hunter must have noticed his dismay. "Toughen up, ole boy," Cunningham said, lightly. "You'll get accustomed to it soon enough."

Kevin nodded, acquiescing. But he thought a body needed rest before acclimating to new labor. The hunters ambled away before Kevin had the rifles fully situated on his shoulders. They headed out of a wooded area toward the center of the large park. Niles extinguished the lantern, but didn't tuck it away into the knapsack. It swung in unison with each step he took.

"That grate suggests the Rhino-pards didn't surface here," Niles said.

"Definitely not," Cunningham agreed. "And there wasn't any sign of them browsing through the brush either. The beasts hadn't even tried that pipe."

"But we're close to the locations of various attacks."

"Indeed," said Cunningham. "They're bedding in the catacombs beneath this very park. Although the attacks have been relatively close by, I expect the beasts are surfacing at a few access points."

They stepped out of a cluster of trees and the expansive park came into view. Kevin noticed people frolicking on the lawn. Some appeared to be students sprawled out on blankets studying. A few others were young professionals picnicking in town. Everyone was formally dressed. The girls wore dresses and the guys had vested wool suits. Even the students wore suit jackets.

Red and white checked blankets were spread out with picnic baskets on top; some of the baskets were made of wicker and others comprised of bamboo sheets meshed together.

Kevin noticed some picnickers sipping glasses of wine, and others drank coffee from plaid thermoses. Pathways ran throughout the park, crowded with pedestrians headed to appointments, errands, or taking advantage of a beautiful day. Everything appeared tranquil, a crisp and sunny fall afternoon. Serene.

"Why don't we just get more men and drive them out?" Kevin said. "And then have us waiting at the access points."

"Blazes!" Cunningham shouted, turning toward Kevin. "What on earth gave you that idea?"

"We have deer drives in Maine all the time," he explained. "You send a wave of hunters into the marsh and swampy areas during the day when the deer are bedding. They walk a line and drive the deer toward awaiting hunters."

"You have hunters shooting toward the men driving the deer?" Cunningham quipped. "How bloody awful."

"We do it all the time," Kevin replied meekly. "You just have to be careful. Besides, the men driving here would be safe in the tunnels."

"But not very safe from the Rhino-pards down there," Niles commented.

Kevin shrugged. So, even they were thinking the big bore rifles might have issues taking the beasts down. These experienced hunters had their own doubts. A shudder of dread ran through him.

"The kid potentially has a point," Niles said to Cunningham.

Surprisingly, the Great Hunter nodded in agreement. "This is true," he said. "My concern is with having too many points of egress. The beasts could get out any which way and wreak havoc in the city."

"You'd have to track all the access points down and seal them off except for one."

"That would prevent them from getting loose in the city." Cunningham chortled. "And it would direct the beasts to our awaiting rifles, rather than chance them happening upon the 10th Hussars!"

Niles snickered at the comment. "We'd need to ensure that our rifles can take these creatures down. And there would have to be safety precautions for the driving team in the tunnels."

"Right you are, chap," said Cunningham, rubbing his chin. "Haven't got that last part figured out yet."

"Neither have I, especially given our experience down there."

"True, very true," Cunningham replied. "A hunter can walk right upon these creatures with little notice. The driving party could easily be turned into a slaughter party."

Niles looked grim. "Must give it a little more thought."

"Indeed, we're just getting a handle on the situation. Now what are we going to do about the Rover?"

"The Rover is about three clicks from here," Niles said. "We can just force-march it over there."

Kevin was taken aback by the comment. The last thing he wanted to do was tote the rifles all the way back. They were close to the quarters, and so he'd hoped to stop and unload the gear. Then, he caught Niles looking over his shoulder. The slender hunter winked and grinned.

Cunningham seemed to get wind of the shenanigans. "What in Pete's sake is the plan, lads?"

Niles shrugged. "Well, I was thinking that—"

The hunters came to an abrupt halt. Kevin spotted the issue and unslung the rifles, then turned them over to awaiting hands. Frozen, neither of them turned to look at the weapons. They instinctively grabbed the stocks and slowly brought their rifles to port arms.

Kevin saw the Rhino-pards standing at the edge of the brush line. The beasts twitched their prodigious feline nostrils, picking up a scent. Nobody else in the park seemed to have noticed them. He figured the hunters were being careful not to send the beasts into a charge. The hunters began to slowly ease their way toward a point, midway between the creatures and their prey.

Moving downwind, the hunters kept a watchful eye on the beasts. The Rhino-pards didn't pick up the scent of the hunters, nor did they appear to sense any danger.

Kevin wasn't sure if he should follow after them, or remain behind. He didn't want to be the cause of alerting the Rhino-pards to the hunt. So he didn't move. As Niles and Cunningham ventured further away, Kevin began to worry that his presence might attract the creatures' attention. He was alone on a slight hillside, almost in line with the beasts.

Then, the Rhino-pard with a blood-stained maw, eased from the wood line. The large creature almost slinked forward. It stopped after moving forward a few meters. The moist nose twitched faster. Its hind legs rippled massive muscles.

The beast was extremely intense, as though it was ready to pounce.

When the companion stepped from the woods, it took up a position half a meter behind the lead Rhino-pard. The second beast grew tense staring at the picnickers. It snorted and dug a paw at the ground.

A few of the picnickers finally noticed the beasts and became frantic. Some began packing up the baskets, while others started fleeing the park.

Both Rhino-pards snorted and scraped at the ground. The people in flight stirred the beasts on. Cunningham and Niles picked up their pace to a trot. Kevin caught a glimpse of dire concern on the Great Hunter's face.

A man lay in the grass reading a newspaper. When the man finally registered the commotion, he stood up screaming. Panic cut through the air.

"That's it," Cunningham railed. "They're going to charge!"

The first Rhino-pard lunged forward, tearing up dried grass. A cloud of dust trailed behind its massive hind legs. Then, the other beast followed in the pursuit.

Cunningham and Niles broke into a mad dash.

The beasts charged. Within seventy-five meters of their prey, they closed in fast. The hunters were farther away and Cunningham's chubby legs only carried him so fast. Kevin decided to make a break for the action.

He watched in horror as the lead Rhino-pard ducked its head, and rammed into the man with the newspaper. The large horn impaled his abdomen. With a flick of its massive neck, the creature discarded the kill. The man tumbled into the grass with the glassy eyes of death already upon him. Blood gushed from the enormous stomach wound.

The two beasts continued their charge, stamping over picnic baskets and shattering place-settings. Kevin approached the hunters; a pained, hopeless look was cast on Cunningham's face. As the Rhino-pards stampeded toward a crowd of fleeing park goers, the beats lowered their heads and readied the fierce horns.

Cunningham looked at Niles in desperation. Kevin understood the situation was dire. A missed shot with the big bore rifles could kill someone by accident. The Rhino-pards were closing in fast.

The hunters dropped to their knees and raised the rifles.

The creatures were swift and quickly ran among the crowd. They tilted their heads from side to side, piercing the deadly horns into people. They cast the wounded prey to the side, and quickly set their sights on another, trampling over fallen bodies.

The Rhino-pards cleared through the crowd angling to circle back. Cunningham and Niles shouldered the rifles and took aim. They now had clear shots at the beasts without endangering the throng of fleeing pedestrians.

Until the 10th Hussars rushed in on horseback, galloping between the beasts and the crowd. The mounted soldiers blocked the beasts from Cunningham and Niles. A flurry of commotion disrupted the hunt.

"Blazes!" Cunningham stood and threw his hat on the ground.

"This isn't going to be pretty," Niles said, shaking his head. "They've no idea of what these beasts are capable of."

"The 10th Hussars will ruin this opportunity," Cunningham shouted. "Absolutely ruin our chances here."

Niles shook his head again as Kevin caught up with them. Both of the hunters had grave looks on their faces, watching the fracas in the distance. The park goers came to a standstill, almost corralled behind the cavalry.

As the Rhino-pards came around, and squared off against the 10th Hussars, the soldiers readied their Lee-Enfield rifles. They shouldered the brown stocks and worked the bolts to chamber the first round. Kevin knew they held repeating rifles with ten rounds in each magazine. He figured the soldiers could deter the beasts if they got assembled in time.

Horses pranced and bayed, as the soldiers steadied the line. Their commanding officer sat proudly in his saddle, brandishing a cutlass. "Steady!" he shouted. "Steady, now!"

The Rhino-pards sized up the 10th Hussars. The pause took long enough for the soldiers to get into formation. They lined up gloriously. Each horse stood planted side by side, while the soldiers pressed their boots into the stirrups and leveled their rifles.

Cunningham turned to Niles and Kevin lifting his eyebrows. "We might not be out of this yet. Come, we'll set up a defensive position."

As the three of them ran to a point behind the crowd of pedestrians, the Rhino-pards snorted and began to charge. They drove headlong into the line of horses. The Enfield rifles cracked off powerful .303 rounds, but the bullets registered little impact on the beasts.

Feline ears pinned back and sharp horns ready to strike, the Rhino-pards charged at the center of the line. Horses reared. A few horsemen were thrown to the ground. Rifles continued to fire and spent gunpowder wafted through the air.

The beasts broke through the line and rushed at scattering pedestrians.

Tilting their heads down, the Rhino-pards thrust their horns into the helpless prey. Blood splattered as people were impaled and trampled. The lead Rhino-pard thrashed its muzzle, gnawing on flailing arms and legs, sinking its fangs into the fallen. The skirmish had turned into a slaughter. Soldiers fired weapons that didn't affect the Rhino-pards, and park goers stood little chance of survival.

Soon, the creatures tore through the crowd. They pounded the grass, kicking dirt and dust into the air, while circling around to make another pass.

Cunningham and Niles dropped to a knee, shouldered their rifles, and flicked off their safeties. Without speaking, Cunningham aimed at the Rhino-pard in the lead, and Niles sighted in on the other.

Each big bore rifle let out a powerful- KABOOM. The Weatherby bullet hit the shoulder of the lead Rhino-pard and the Gibbs shot a round into the side of its companion. Kevin noticed the shoulder dip slightly after the lead beast got hit. The other creature reflected a mild discomfort at the shot into its hide. As the hunters steadied their rifles to squeeze off another round, the beasts turned to face them.

The creature in the lead had crimson smeared around its mouth. The Rhino-pards snorted and shook their heads, snapping their chins toward the ground in defiance. The lead beast clawed the ground, sending a clump of grass flying. The other gave the earth a quick swipe. Then they charged, building up steam, marking their pursuit.

Cunningham held his breath and took steady aim. KABOOM! The Weatherby sent a round into the opposite shoulder of the lead Rhino-pard. Niles fired the Gibbs and hit the trailing Rhino-pard in a shoulder. The rifle blasts rung Kevin's ears. He could barely hear Cunningham, but caught a mumbled: "Go for the same shoulder."

The hunters fired again. Rounds hit home, sinking into the wounded shoulders. A greenish fluid oozed from the marred shoulder of the lead Rhino-pard. The beast's gait let up. The rifle shots impeded the attack, but the creatures continued a staggered charge at the hunters.

"Fire again!" Cunningham wailed.

The beasts closed in fast. Heavy feet thumped over the grass and fierce determination shone in their golden eyes.

"They're coming!" Cunningham shouted.

Niles had trouble with his bolt. A round popped up slightly crooked, failing to chamber. The Weatherby let out another loud crack. Cunningham hit the lead Rhino-pard in the same shoulder a third time. The right front leg wavered as though the creature might drop.

The Rhino-pards closed within ten paces. By the time Niles got his next round chambered, the Rhino-pards were upon them.

Shoulder wounds impaired the lead beast, causing it to stumble. It cantered to the side of the Great Hunter. The Rhino-pard thundered past Cunningham, a gust blowing his hair and mustache. A haunch collided with Kevin and sent him soaring into the air.

He landed on the ground, catching a glimpse of the other Rhino-pard. The beast drove headlong into Niles. Its horn caught under the hunter's abdomen and flung him upward. Niles hurled through the air and fell on the grass in a crumpled ball.

The beasts circled around for another strike. But the 10th Hussars rushed upon the scene with Enfield rifles blazing. The Rhino-pards trampled off, making a final sweep through the melee. Biting into limbs, the beasts snatched up fallen pedestrians, then dragged off their spoils toward the wood line.

Dazed, Kevin watched in awe as the creatures' hind ends slipped into dense foliage and out of sight.

CHAPTER THIRTEEN

Lying in the grass, Kevin felt lightheaded, and disoriented. Commotion nearby sounded muffled, surreal. He glanced up. Through foggy vision, he saw soldiers tending to the wounded. The macabre scene resembled a battlefield, similar to images of frontline troops decimated by cannon fire.

He looked over at Niles, crumpled in the grass. Blood splattered the hunter's tan shooting jacket. Cunningham knelt by his fallen comrade, looking sullen.

Kevin rose and approached them meekly. He didn't want to intrude at a delicate time, so he stood a few meters away. The situation looked grim. Both hunters had served together in combat and on hunting expeditions for decades. Anguish exuded from Cunningham's eyes.

"Don't think I'm going to pull through on this one," Niles muttered.

"Rubbish," Cunningham retorted. "Absolute rubbish!"

Niles smiled gently. "I'm afraid so. The beast really did a number on me. My insides are broken up for sure."

Cunningham shook his head solemnly. He noticed Kevin for the first time, and locked eyes with the young gun bearer. Reproach gleamed from the Great Hunter's stare. Kevin wondered if Cunningham blamed him for the incident.

Maybe he thought the rounds hadn't been loaded correctly, or dirt had gotten on a cartridge and prevented it from chambering properly. Either way, Niles hadn't been able to get a shot off, and the Rhino-pard trampled him. Kevin had been the gun bearer.

After a moment, Kevin snatched the Gibbs from the ground and took off toward the wood line.

"Wait, lad," Cunningham bellowed. "It's too risky!"

"Don't worry about me," Kevin called over his shoulder. "Take care of Niles, and I'll be back later."

Entering the woods, Kevin immediately picked up their trail. The beasts had obviously trampled over the same ground a number of times. A distinct path led through the brush. He figured an access point was nearby.

Pieces of bloodied clothing had snagged on branches. It didn't take an experienced hunter to track the creatures through the woods. Kevin's boots squished into muddy ground. A rivulet ran across the path, so he figured a pipe opening lay ahead.

Kevin worked the bolt chambering a round, and then he wrapped the sling tightly around his left forearm. He stepped carefully over the dried pine needles and scanned for the beasts. For some reason, he didn't put it past them to linger in the dense brush, waiting to pounce on whoever approached the entrance to their den.

The sloshing of his boots over muddy terrain sent a shiver through his body. Kevin expected a Rhino-pard to hear his approach and charge. A twig snapped. Panic raced through his veins.

Beginning to question why he'd ventured out alone, Kevin saw sunlight reflecting off the steel access pipe. Metal grating, twisted, was flung open from the mouth of the pipe.

****

Stepping inside, Kevin began to reconsider the wisdom of his pursuit. Light only cast into the pipeline five to six meters. The pipe had been inserted into an antiquated brick passageway approximately half of that distance.

He paused, trying to adjust his eyes to the darkness. Everything beyond the span of daylight remained black. Kevin moved a little further into the tunnel, but still couldn't see anything beyond a ten-meter arc of daylight. The Rhino-pards could be lying in wait, lurking in the shadows.

Kevin treaded forward carefully. His boots sloshed in six centimeters of water, running through the tunnel. The noise caused him to halt abruptly. Listening for the sound of Rhino-pard feet splashing, he only heard an occasional drip; it was the sound of groundwater meandering into crevices in the old mortar. Otherwise, the catacombs remained silent.

He listened again for thuds of massive feet pounding through the tunnel. Kevin craned his neck trying to hear snorts, or heavy breathing from the beasts. Nothing. The tunnel remained still, except for the intermittent drips. He held the Gibbs with the safety off, ready to fire.

Moving ahead, he nervously stepped from the demarcation of daylight into blackness. Kevin's eyes took a moment to adjust. Nothing jumped out at him. And he soon realized that only an empty tunnel lay ahead.

An intersecting passageway lay five meters ahead. Kevin shouldered the rifle and slowly approached.

He reached the intersecting tunnel, pausing to look around. The passageway had become darker. Turning down either side tunnel would immediately lead to pitch blackness. Kevin eased against a tunnel wall and then stepped around a corner.

The area was clear of the beasts. He could see less than three meters away and realized the expedition was hindered without a lantern. Kevin slumped regretfully and turned to leave, his boots kicking up water.

Splashing echoed through the catacombs.

More splashes, heavy and close by, caused him to stop. Then, a paw shot from the darkness and struck him in the back. He flew forward and crashed to the deck. The Gibbs fell from his hands. Kevin scrambled for the rifle, but met a set of menacing golden eyes.

He froze, locking glances with yellow orbs, peering through the darkness. The Rhino-pard roared and swatted the rifle away.

Long fangs shown in the scant light, dripping saliva, as the creature slinked its massive bulk closer. Kevin squirmed away, kicking his legs and pedaling his arms.

The Rhino-pard slowly eased forward, toying with its prey. Kevin felt helpless, as though flight was meager and futile.

As the beast moved closer, Kevin smelt its fetid breath. The stench of its victims drifted through the tunnel. Kevin wormed away from the creature, until a paw pressed down on his ankle. Smears of crimson stained the fur around its mouth.

Pain shot into his leg from the weight of the creature. Kevin tried to wiggle his foot free, but the beast had him pinned. A mere slight pressing on his lower leg had completely immobilized him. The Rhino-pard almost seemed to wink sardonically.

An ache in his back reminded Kevin of the Ray-gun. He reached around to the rear of his trousers and extracted the weapon. Holding the bizarre gun, futuristic, but antiquated, he now feared it being only a toy.

Fumbling to find a safety, Kevin knew he had little time. The beast canted its massive head. The horn tilted and the feline eyes blinked, almost nervously.

The creature snorted and let out a roar.

Panic raced through Kevin's body. He couldn't find any sign of a safety mechanism. The Rhino-pard tensed and leapt into the air.

Kevin pointed the Ray-gun at the beast.

He squeezed the trigger.

A red beam shot from the barrel, striking the beast in the chest. Kevin rolled to the side. The Rhino-pard yowled in pain, splashing into the water as it landed hard next to him.

Kevin backpedaled from the fallen creature. The beast winced, trying to get its bearings. Turning its head toward Kevin, the Rhino-pard let out a growling hiss, then rose to its feet on shaking legs. The beast slinked forward a couple of steps, gently stalking its prey. Kevin knew that it would attack again.

He pointed the Ray-gun at the creature, but feared pulling the trigger. Another painful blow might send the beast into a bloody tirade.

The Rhino-pard lunged without warning.

Firing the Ray-gun, he shot another beam of red light into the beast's chest. Then, he got off another blast, hitting the wounded shoulder. The Rhino-pard wailed in pain. Stopping in its tracks, the beast snorted, and slowly backed away.

Kevin held the Ray-gun ready to fire again. He didn't think the gun would drop the beast if it charged; it would maul him to death, so he remained still, watching it retreat.

Soon, the beast backed out of sight. Kevin stared into the darkness, worried that its companion would step forth. He didn't waste any time. Sticking the Ray-gun into his trousers, Kevin scooped up the Gibbs and darted for the access pipe.

He reached daylight and sprinted into the woods. Kevin made it partway down the path and tripped on a root. He fell, cracking his head on a rock. Vision blurring, he nestled on a bed of pine needles, and lost consciousness.

CHAPTER FOURTEEN

Sarah sat in a wing chair listening to Cunningham, as Kevin lay on the floor sound asleep. He eventually stirred from his slumbers. Awaking to a crackling fire and light banter, Kevin lifted his head from a stupor. His body clearly ached and his vision seemed blurry. He squinted and glanced around looking dumbfounded, as though it took him a moment to realize they were back at the quarters.

Kevin was strewn on a bedroll with his head nestled into Cunningham's gear. He glanced toward her Victorian dress, draping from a wingchair; he looked up at Sarah, appearing as though her presence comforted him.

"Look who has finally joined us," Cunningham quipped.

Laughter spread throughout the room. "He's been a tired boy," Sarah said. "You must not keep him engaged for prolonged periods of time."

"Afraid we tired the lad out today," Cunningham admitted.

Kevin seemed puzzled at not finding a melancholy crew. Instead, they were a jovial bunch carrying on as though tragedy hadn't forsaken them. Then, he seemed to sense a nervous hesitation to their comments, as though trying to cope with a horrible situation. He sat up slightly and glanced at Cunningham holding a glass of whiskey.

The Great Hunter caught Kevin glancing at the whiskey. Cunningham perused his Old-Fashioned glass and shrugged. "Suppose that you should have one of these as well," said Cunningham.

"What about Niles?" Kevin rebuked. "We can't just sit around laughing and drinking whiskey."

"Why, Niles has his own glass," Cunningham chuckled.

Kevin froze and peered out of the corner of his eye. The other hunter lay strewn across the Chippendale sofa. A pillow propped him up enough to imbibe in the colonial spirits. He held his glass up to Kevin and smiled. "Cheers!"

Sarah noticed Kevin's eyes growing wide. Everyone laughed and sipped their whiskey, including Sarah. He looked at her amazed.

"What?" she rebuffed. "A lady is perfectly entitled to indulge a little."

Kevin turned his palms upward, not sure how to respond.

"Here you go, my lad," Cunningham said, handing over a drink.

Sitting up, Kevin winced as pain shot through his left side. He reached over and touched his ribs. Bandages were wrapped around his torso. He took the drink and glanced at Cunningham, apparently searching the hunter's eyes for answers.

"We got you patched up in a jiffy," Cunningham said. "The beast got a good swipe at you down in the tunnel."

Kevin looked at him surprised.

"Don't worry. We got the wounds all cleaned out."

"Wounds?" Kevin questioned. "Don't even recall getting injured."

"Happens all the time," Niles interjected. "The adrenaline is pumping so you don't feel the extent of the injury until later. The whiskey will help now that you've come around, though."

"How about you?" Kevin wondered aloud. "Did you feel the rhino horn right away?"

"Bollocks!" Niles hollered. "That's the type of thing that you feel immediately, son. And suffer with long afterward. Now, isn't that right, Silas?"

"Mighty true," Cunningham replied. "This is most definitely the case. Why an injury like that strikes the pain sensors right away. Recuperation takes months. And the warrior is left with aches and pain for a lifetime."

Kevin took a long sip of his whiskey. "So, I should consider myself lucky."

"Consider yourself *damn* lucky," Niles said, lifting his glass again. "You're fortunate to have gotten out of the tunnels alive."

"Most fortunate indeed," Cunningham added. "Not sure of the wisdom in heading down there alone. But it sure took some gumption."

Kevin sipped his drink and seemed to quietly ponder the events in the park. The beasts had caused havoc, killing innocent people and maiming others. Sarah suspected that he couldn't quite shake the bloody carnage from his mind.

Cunningham seemed to notice his ruminations too. "Drink up, son. There'll be better days ahead of you."

"Sure thing," Kevin said, taking a sip. "What happened to everyone?"

"Lost two soldiers and three civilians," Cunningham replied. "Many others are in hospital. Some are severely wounded and we're not sure if a few of them will pull through."

"Considering the havoc the Rhino-pards had caused," Niles added, "things might have been a lot worse."

Running the events through her mind, Sarah couldn't think of much else they could have done. She started to wonder if tracking in the tunnels had been careless. Maybe they drove the beasts to stampede in the park.

Kevin polished off the drink and propped against the bedroll. He glanced toward Sarah appearing despondent. Despair overcame him. Perhaps the thought of being partly responsible for the deaths and catastrophic injuries to others was daunting. And he had to feel horrible for those that were injured and would live with the fiasco the rest of their lives.

Sarah wanted to climb down from the chair and scoot across the floor and comfort him. The drink seemed to buzz Kevin's head. He sat still as if longing for something. She knew that her life demanded that people act like adults, take risk, and endure suffering. Sarah wondered if Kevin lived in a world that was merely a protected shell.

Aside from rare acts of violence, accidents, and random wild animals, he might never have to think about harm, or pain and loss, especially loss suffered on account of his shortcomings and failures. Life in her city was clearly more daunting.

Maybe he hadn't loaded the Gibbs properly, she thought.

Niles might not have been injured, and perhaps the Rhino-pards wouldn't have taken a last pass through the crowd. He could be thinking something like that, anyway, even if it were not the case. Kevin seemed to have the weight of the world on his shoulders.

"Don't beat yourself up about it, lad," Cunningham finally said, as though reading her mind. "There was nothing more that could've been done out there. These beasts are very keen. Nothing like what we've ever gone after in the past."

Niles struggled to sit up. "Indeed, the Frenchman has really outdone himself this time. Those creatures are scientifically enhanced, brutishly strong but agile. And very smart."

"Very smart, indeed," Cunningham added.

"Who is this Frenchman anyway?" Kevin demanded.

"Doctor Jean Priolet," said Niles. "A most brilliant and disturbing scientist."

"So, you've come across him before?"

"Most certainly." Niles sipped his whiskey. "He's been involved in an assortment of shady dealings, and some of them have involved questionable scientific experiments. But nothing quite like this. This is the work of a diabolic and most depraved mind."

"Certainly a depraved man," Cunningham agreed. "And heavens no, we've never encountered anything quite like this before. Nothing like this at all, in fact."

"The intellect of those creatures sets them apart," Niles continued. "That may be the most significant difference."

The Great Hunter waved his hands to everyone. "Let's get the boy something to eat. Shall we?"

And with that, Sarah rang the bell for Alice.

****

Later, nibbling on a sandwich, Kevin sat quietly, listening to the hunters talk about various tracking methods. After some discourse, Niles eventually threw his hands up in frustration.

"Silas, I am not sure the precise tracking method is going to matter."

"Why on heavens not?" said Cunningham.

"What are we going to do once we get the beasts pinned down? Our weapons don't really seem to work on them."

Cunningham rubbed his chin. "Sure, sure. I see your point there. A most troubling situation. Most troubling, indeed."

The room fell silent. Kevin listened to the crackling fire and glanced around at the artwork, paneled walls, and high ceilings.

The sandwich tasted good and helped settle his stomach from the whiskey. Cunningham helped himself to a third sandwich. Kevin suspected the hunter already had a few while he was asleep on the floor.

"Well, I have an idea," Sarah said, breaking the silence. "My thought is that we should trap the creatures."

Kevin noticed that her eyes lit up proudly. She smiled at him and he felt a twinge of warmth.

"Blazes, what in heaven is the girl talking about?" Cunningham bellowed.

"She is suggesting that we trap the beasts, instead of plotting to take them down in the field," Niles explained. "Not the sort of approach we've taken in the past."

"We couldn't possibly trap them," Cunningham said, quizzically. "I can't think of a trap that would hold the beasts. And that certainly wouldn't be hunting."

"Well, I thought that your charge was to destroy these horrible creatures in order to prevent them from causing havoc in the city," Sarah said, as she adjusted her dress and pouted, discontentedly. "There most certainly is a way to trap them. Just like capturing a grizzly bear. Hunters in our wild west dig large pits and cover them with brush. The bears fall into the pits and are taken down inside them."

"We'd have to build large pits and find a way to get them to fall in," said Cunningham. "These creatures are smart and might not fall for it. And we'll have the same issue once they're trapped. How do we kill them?"

Niles grinned confidently. "Well, this gives me an idea. But we'll have to consult with the Royal Society of Steam and Power-Plant Engineers."

****

After Niles detailed the plan, Sarah sat quiet sipping tea. Kevin lay back on the bedroll. He folded his hands behind his head, intent to catch up on needed rest. Cunningham would definitely work him hard before the day was done.

"Sounds like we've got ourselves a plan," Cunningham said, pouring two fingers of whiskey. "Mighty good stuff. Your colonies have surely done something right."

"That and tobacco," Niles added. "The cigars from the Virginia and Carolina colonies are profound."

"Why thank you," Sarah replied. "We try to pride ourselves on the various strong points that each colony has to offer. You should try some of the shellfish that come from our Massachusetts Bay Colony while on your visit."

"Your companionship and guidance are much appreciated," Cunningham said to Sarah. "This hunt is such a major endeavor that we've little time to consider such particulars as where to dine."

Sarah flashed a coy smile. "Gentlemen, I would be most honored to accompany you to dinner this evening. After we discuss a few further details about *our* hunt."

"Now, it's *our* hunt," Cunningham repeated, slightly alarmed. "I dare say, how did that come to being?"

"Why, with Niles laid up," Sarah explained, "it only makes sense that a strong woman joins in this most sordid affair. Those atrocious beasts must be put to rest for the public good."

She patted the edge of her dress as though there was nothing left to discuss. Cunningham raised his eyebrows, dismissing the idea of a debate without heated discussion. Sarah noticed that Niles seemed to ruminate over the prospect of having her join the hunting party. This wasn't lost on the Great Hunter.

"What is it my man?" Cunningham demanded. "Out with it!"

Niles nudged his elbow into the sofa, sitting up to look directly at Cunningham. He took a moment to gather his breath before speaking.

"Well, pray tell us what you have in mind?" Cunningham insisted.

"My recollection of the Rhino-pards," said Niles candidly, "both in the tunnels and on the field today, suggests that they prefer feminine prey."

Cunningham's eyes stretched wide in obvious protest. "You're not suggesting that we use the girl as bait, are you?"

"Heavens no," Niles replied, snickering. "I dare say that we use both of them."

"Blazes!" Cunningham stormed. "That's the worst possible idea I've heard yet."

Sarah calmly patted her hands upon the sides of her dress. "Well, I am the only person to survive an attack by the beasts… at least until today," she offered.

The room dropped into a lull of unsettled silence. All three men apparently sensed her dismay, and turned toward her. They seemed to anticipate that she'd make a bold statement, but they were utterly unprepared for what she had to say.

"Niles makes perfect sense," Sarah finally expostulated. "Something needs to be done to lure the beasts into our deadly trap. We are perfectly capable of standing our own in the face of the horrible creatures. And there is no reason why our lives should be put before the lovely compatriots who are constantly at risk about the city."

"Well, I guess that settles it," Niles said, cheerfully.

Cunningham shrugged, defeated at the hands of Sarah's wit and determination. He swallowed the remainder of his whiskey in a single gulp.

"Besides," Niles continued, "the two of you have a distinct advantage over others."

Kevin looked toward the injured hunter perplexed. "What on earth do you mean?"

Putting the whiskey glass on the tea table, Cunningham stood and stepped over to his gear. He reached behind a pile of equipment. "I mean this," Cunningham said, holding out the Ray-gun.

Kevin hadn't noticed that something was missing from his person, even though he seemed a lot more comfortable lounging on his back than he'd appeared earlier in the day. With all of the commotion and surprise, it hadn't registered that something was gone. Cunningham's eyes were lit up in excitement.

"What do you say, lad?" Cunningham said, mockingly.

Kevin was at a loss for words. A panic engulfed him. The sight of the Ray-gun sent consternation through him, a dismay he didn't seem to quite understand. His face turned color, a complete loss of breath. It was as though Cunningham brandishing the Ray-gun, somehow, had revealed him as a fraud.

"Well, I'd say the boy has gone completely speechless," Niles commented.

Kevin shrugged, obviously not knowing how to respond.

"Come, lad," Cunningham insisted. "Tell us what this is about."

"I really don't know," Kevin said. "It's some kind of weapon."

"Some kind of weapon indeed," Cunningham repeated. "Tell us what you know about it. From the start, son."

"There's not much to tell," Kevin explained. "I was waiting for the inbound train and a man asked me to hold his briefcase. The train arrived and I boarded, but the man never got onboard. I found that in the briefcase and some clothes. That's about it."

"Those clothes suit you well, lad," Cunningham said. "Except for that hairdo from the Orient, you fit right in around here."

"So, the weapon was in the portmanteau that you brought in here," Niles clarified. "And the suitcase was filled with clothing tailor-fitted to you?"

"That may seem odd," Kevin conceded. "But I do have an average build. So, it is not surprising that the clothes fit."

"Are you saying that the weapon doesn't belong to you?" Cunningham griped.

"That's exactly what I'm saying."

"Who did you get it from?" Niles questioned.

"A man named Roland. He was on the platform for the inbound train."

"Rubbish!" Cunningham hollered. "Absolute rubbish! That weapon doesn't belong to anyone but you."

Kevin raised his hands, pleading.

"The boy obviously doesn't comprehend," Niles suggested to the Great Hunter. "Seems entirely ignorant of many things, including the Ray-gun."

Cunningham nodded. "Indeed, he's absolutely ignorant. Or playing us for fools."

"I'm telling you the truth," Kevin protested. "The Ray-gun belonged to a man named Roland."

"There he goes again," Cunningham said, throwing up his hands.

"Why don't you believe me?"

"Because we know that you fired the Ray-gun in the tunnels."

"So, I admit that."

"See, he admits it," Cunningham quipped.

"But the weapon doesn't belong to me—"

"We know," Cunningham muttered, "it belongs to this *Roland* fellow. Rubbish!"

Kevin turned to Niles. "I'm telling the truth, honestly."

"You can't be telling the truth, lad," Niles said. "How can you admit to firing it, but then claim that it belongs to this Roland chap?"

"That's precisely what happened."

"Rubbish!" Cunningham ground his teeth. "The weapon cannot belong to anybody but you."

"Why do you keep saying that?"

"Because you bloody well know," Cunningham yelled, waving his arms. "You fired the blasted thing."

"So?" Kevin questioned. "I don't understand."

"Only the rightful owner of a Ray-gun can fire it," Niles replied, grinning.

Sarah shook her head in dismay. The boy sounded too naive to be telling anything but the truth. She just hoped that he had the stuff to carry out the plan. His protested ignorance was confirming her belief that he'd come from somewhere a lot cushier than Massachusetts Bay.

CHAPTER FIFTEEN

Floating high above the city in a two-man airship, Kevin scanned for possible access points in which the Rhino-pards could surface from tunnels. He used a long telescope. The extended tubes and eyepieces were brass, but the main housing was wrapped in hand-stenciled teak veneer.

Cunningham stood beside him, manning the air balloon. The Great Hunter's pudgy face was squeezed into a pair of brass goggles. His walrus mustache fluttered in the breeze. Cunningham obviously enjoyed flying the airship, cackling at the control stick. Kevin could hardly keep the telescope focused. The Great Hunter sailed the airship along, swaying the basket from side to side, as he navigated it through the sky.

"Cheer up, lad," Cunningham jibed. "This could be a lot worse, so you might as well make the best of it. Try to enjoy the ride."

Kevin nodded. "But we're out here to get a job done, and I can hardly focus with the balloon swaying back and forth."

"Airship," Cunningham chided him. "How many times do I have to tell you… it's a bloody airship. Self-propelled and all."

The airship looked similar to hot air balloons from Kevin's world, except the basket protruded at the front and came equipped with a steam boiler in the rear. It had an iron cylinder stoked with coal for heating air in the balloon. A long tube ran to a burner above them. Cunningham occasionally reached overhead and pulled on a platinum handle. A flame roared and heated the air, raising the balloon higher.

The airship had a peculiar engineering aspect that Kevin couldn't understand. A propeller was attached to the rear by intricate wooden buttresses that ran up to a brass ring at the base of the balloon. The propeller appeared to be solid mahogany.

Even as it spun through the air, Kevin noticed a shiny laminate, as though it was well kept. A rudder extended from the rear of the basket and a control stick jutted from the basket floor, similar to bi-planes used in the Great War. The entire airship was immaculate, not unlike the steam train he'd ridden on.

Kevin used the long telescope to search for signs of the Rhino-pards. He understood the beasts would exit the tunnels beneath the city, and so he knew enough to scan areas adjacent to established infrastructure.

Blueprints of the underground systems fluttered in the breeze. Kevin used them to determine where the steam lines ran. All the piping went through tunnels, so he had a good idea where the passageways were located. By confining his search to the adjacent areas near the park, he'd narrowed the effort. Some of the tunnels ran beneath streets and under buildings.

Despite the pilot's antics, Kevin was able to spot a few paths leading from heavily wooded areas in the park, and a few occasional embankments located near open lots, overpasses, and railway bridges.

He marked up the blueprints with a colored pencil. They had passed the major strategic points a few times circling around the city. Kevin gave it a last, hasty scan. Everything seemed to be documented as well as he could expect.

Turning toward Cunningham, he rolled up the blueprints and collapsed the telescope. "Think we've got it."

"Well, hold on then," Cunningham said, driving the stick to the left. "We've got to make another pass around, for good-time's sake!"

"What?" Kevin responded, being thrown about the basket.

"Hold on, lad," Cunningham chirped. "You haven't got your sea legs yet."

The airship took another pass over the city. Cunningham made sure to make a grand play of it all. He cut the rudder back and forth, gliding the airship through the sky. Maneuvering the vessel at a brisk speed, he dived toward the park, buzzing pedestrians, and then whipped it back around the trees.

Zipping along, Kevin was unable to utilize the spyglass. But he strained to make every effort to continue his surveillance.

"Just sit back and enjoy the ride, lad," Cunningham hooted.

Kevin was about to relax when he noticed something. "Wait! Take us by there again," he said, pointing to a clump of trees.

Cunningham worked the stick and pulled the handle releasing more hot air. The airship rose up and swung around. Kevin leaned over the basket with the spyglass in hand. A small grove of trees stood on the edge of the park. He'd focused on the large track of wooded area in the center of the common and overlooked the small cluster of trees.

This smaller grove of trees didn't seem like a suitable access point. It was close to intersecting streets at the edge of the park and afforded scant coverage to conceal the beasts coming and going. Yet, matted grass led into the grove, trampled by something heavy.

Kevin postulated that Rhino-pards had worn the grass down. However, he began to consider that it could merely be a shortcut through the park.

"What is it, son?" Cunningham snapped, as the basket rocked. "I can't hold this position steady much longer."

"We can move on," Kevin replied. Then, he knelt down and pulled out the blueprints, marking the location as a possibility. Cunningham maneuvered the airship through the sky, cutting back and forth. Kevin shifted from side to side, holding the basket tightly to keep from being tossed about, as the Great Hunter cackled with joy at Kevin's discomfort.

Finally, the airship lowered to a landing field. Cunningham carefully brought it to rest near a mast protruding from the ground. He nodded to Kevin, who alighted from the basket and tethered the ship to the wooden support.

"That was a fine bit of intelligence we gathered," Cunningham said, pulling his goggles on top of his head.

Kevin reached into the basket and grabbed the marked-up drawings. "Hopefully, we've got their habitat pinned down."

"Most likely have all of the access points identified," Cunningham offered. "Just hope the plan works out. Mighty dangerous. Mighty dangerous, indeed."

A sinking feeling overcame Kevin's spirits. He'd seen the resolve of the Rhino-pards and wondered if the plan could be carried out without further carnage. He dreaded the thought of dying in this strange world.

****

After reconnoitering the potential access points from the sky, Kevin and Cunningham took to the ground and carefully inspected the sundry locations that he'd marked on the blueprints.

The 10th Hussars set up a barricade on the far side of the park, just beyond the plain where hunters planned for a skirmish with the beasts. Workers busied themselves welding grates over the access pipes. They secured the new welds by installing timbers to brace the grating.

"The beasts will be quite angry when they happen upon the sealed access points," Cunningham chuckled. "Mighty angry indeed. I expect that when you come upon them, they'll want to take it out on your hide."

Kevin gulped. "Suppose they will. Best double-check the grates to make sure they're secure. Don't want the Rhino-pards to break free somewhere unexpected, and have them circle around on us."

"Nonsense," Cunningham waved him off. "These workers have been supplied by The Corps of Royal Engineers. Not a slacker in the bunch."

"Then, we can head back to the quarters and start on the next step in our plan," Kevin suggested.

"After we replenish our appetite," Cunningham chuckled, elbowing Kevin. "Alice sure makes a decent sandwich."

CHAPTER SIXTEEN

After devouring more sandwiches and a bit of whiskey, Cunningham glanced at Sarah and raised an unbitten half of turkey sandwich. "This bird you have in the New World is excellent. I'm afraid our activities will take us into the night, and so it will have to suffice for dinner."

She feigned a pout. "Missing the opportunity to dine with you all at the Union Oyster House is most disappointing."

"We're sorry as well," Cunningham said, peering toward Kevin. "Some of us are sorrier than others, though."

They all laughed except Kevin. It seemed to take him a moment to get the joke, then he looked uncomfortable. Sarah watched him glance to Niles for help.

"Let's get a move on," Niles said. "We've got a schedule to keep."

"Right you are, my friend." Cunningham stood up and munched down the rest of the sandwich in his hand. "Let's get going, lad."

Kevin and Cunningham hoisted Niles into an oak wheelchair, with rattan seating and backing. Then, the young man wheeled Niles out to the Rover, and stopped at the curb by the front passenger seat. Cunningham barreled past Sarah and assisted in loading the injured hunter into the vehicle. They strapped the wheelchair to the roof and climbed into the back.

Sarah slid behind the wheel. The steam boiler was heated, and the engine rumbled, vibrating the Rover. As soon as the last door closed, she tore down cobblestone roads. Sarah headed toward the outskirts of the financial district, and then drove over the bridge with the plaque commemorating the Boston Tea Party.

They drove across the channel into the rough and tumble of South Boston. Sarah knew her way around the city. She smiled working the levers that controlled the amount of steam chugging from the boiler.

She noticed the terrain unfolding into a vast plain. To the left lay docks and the pipe that the hunters had entered along the shoreline. A few work trucks were parked near the crest of the embankment; all of the trucks were flatbeds with steam pipes jutting from the hoods, and coal bins were fastened to the cabs. The engineers were shoring up the grating, pounding lumber sawed into points, and setting stakes deep into the earth, then pegging beams into the stakes to brace the grates.

Ahead on their right, an immense brick factory stood in grand splendor. Sarah rumbled over cobblestones and pulled onto an expansive brick courtyard.

****

The building reminded Kevin of the mills along the Merrimack River, running from New Hampshire into northern Massachusetts. A prodigious clock tower stood in the center of the building. Wings extended from the tower, standing a few stories tall, with windows running across each floor.

A similar wing extended from the rear of the building, except it had a gable roof with slate shingles, while the side wings had flat rooftops. The rear wing abutted five gigantic smoke stacks set in a row. All of them were brick and each one stood slightly taller than the next.

Sarah brought the Rover to a halt in front of the building. Alighting from the vehicle, Kevin stepped onto a parking lot paved in brick. Something about the building made it appear grand compared to those along the Merrimack Valley in Kevin's world. The clock on the tower seemed similar, Roman numerals and antiquated iron hands, except for a second hand that slowly turned around the immense dial. A smooth circumlocution, it didn't pause with each tick, as though the clock mechanisms were highly refined.

He unstrapped the wheelchair and then Cunningham single-handedly lowered it from the roof. Together, they transferred Niles to the chair. Once Niles settled in, they all gazed upon the factory building in awe.

"Definitely a fine cogeneration steam facility," Niles commented.

"Surely 'tis a nice building," Cunningham muttered. "Now let's get on with it!"

Kevin slowly pushed Niles over the bumpy bricks, while Cunningham made for the front door in haste. Sarah walked alongside the wheelchair, holding up the hem of her skirt to avoid tripping.

The clay bricks on the building looked pristine and the window frames were freshly painted hunter green; the windows that reflected the setting sunlight encompassed a multiple pane technology that hadn't been developed during the industrial revolution of Kevin's world.

Heading to the main door beneath the clock tower, Kevin noticed a sign reading: Bank of England Mills. Somehow, he'd expected the name of a New England manufacturer from industrial days to mark the doorway. A company like Amoskeag Mills or Boott Cotton Mills above the door would have been reassuring. It might have reflected a connection with a past that Kevin understood.

There wasn't a handicap ramp, so Kevin spun the wheelchair around and then jockeyed Niles up the granite steps. He strained to heave the hunter over the stairs. When they reached the landing, Kevin gasped to catch his breath.

Cunningham didn't wait. The Great Hunter bounded over plank flooring, his boots reverberating on the hardwood. "Hurry along now," Cunningham called back.

Kevin exchanged glances with Sarah.

"Why, I'm perfectly willing to lend a hand," said Sarah.

Kevin got behind Niles and pushed off with his legs to get the chair rolling. "That's okay," he replied, "I can handle it."

"Well, I'm surely capable of assisting."

"He knows that," Niles interjected. "We all know that, but the lad feels obligated to carry out his charge. No insult meant to you."

"Thank you," Kevin goaded him. "I couldn't have spoken it better."

"Indeed," Niles agreed. "You colonists are no longer at war with Britain, but you're surely at odds with the Queen's English."

"Some things don't change, no matter where you are," Kevin muttered.

"What's that you say, lad?" Niles tilted his head, looking up at Kevin. "I dare say that you've struck a chord of truth there."

They headed down a long corridor with ceilings five meters high. Cunningham had already disappeared through a doorway at the end of the hall. When they reached the threshold, Kevin stepped into an enormous well-lit room.

Open for three stories, the room had vaulted ceilings with skylights emitting the early evening sun. Rows of windows lined the exterior walls, and much of the floor remained clear, except for a large mechanical device in the center.

Huge columns towered over the room with beams attached at various angles. The framing resembled a medieval siege tower. Inside the timber, giant cogwheels of brass and platinum turned in unison, as though operating a precise machine. The teeth of each gear churned slowly together, a systematic transmission of intricate clockwork.

A disheveled man stood by the mechanism. He wore a tattered top hat, and dusty overcoat. The hat seemed to engulf his small head; sunk down to his ears, the hat was suspended merely by the frames of his spectacles and curly shoulder-length hair. He busied himself reading charts, and didn't seem to notice them approach, despite the pounding of Cunningham's boots.

The Great Hunter cleared his throat, and the man turned to face them. A sardonic grin momentarily flashed on his face. Beady eyes peered through coke-bottle glasses at them.

"You must be my guests," he said, turning kind. "Sent over by The Royal Corps of Engineers. Please do come in and make yourselves comfortable." He forced a smile. "We don't get a lot of visitors here at the plant."

They moved closer. Everyone seemed in awe of the mechanisms, churning behind the man in the large tattered top hat.

"Barney Runge," he said, bowing while tipping his hat. "I'm the Plant Operator."

Cunningham stepped closer. "I'm Silas Cunningham, and this is Niles Barton with our gun bearer, Kevin," he said, pointing. "And we have with us our fair lady friend, Sarah."

Runge looked them all over wide-eyed, a little too enthusiastic. He shuffled toward Niles, glancing with delight. "Niles Barton, the British Architect?"

Niles nodded, smiling modestly. "More of a hunter nowadays."

"Your work on the Royal Palace is legendary. My pleasure to meet you."

A lull in the conversation allowed Kevin to observe the room. Cogs worked in unison, turning a sprocket at the bottom of the gear cluster. Then, a roller chain attached to the sprocket leading to a drive-shaft running through a gap in an interior brick wall.

High on the wall, a magnificent clock ticked with large hands circling an ornate face. It connected to brass cogs that churned gear-teeth together, affixed to platinum arms, joined by smaller cogs; they attached to larger gears, forming a cluster that worked in orderly unison.

Runge clapped his hands together and trundled toward Kevin. "I see you're mystified by our extraordinary clockwork."

"It's most impressive," Kevin replied. "What does it all do?"

"Why, this clockwork serves to run the steam line through the entire city at a constant two-hundred and fifty pounds per square inch," Runge said, turning to face everyone. "The larger apparatus controls the steam pressure. And the clock on the wall sets precise timing for starting up the line, and shutting the system down."

Niles rolled his wheelchair over, getting a better look at the system.

"I'm told that you want to use our line in a most peculiar way," Runge said, feigning a smile. "The very thought of it caused me consternation, but now that I understand Mr. Barton is in your company, perhaps my concerns can be placated."

"We'd like you to slowly shut down the system," Niles explained. "And keep the drip-legs closed at Vault C, located in the common."

"That would allow condensate to collect in the line!" Runge replied, alarmed.

"Precisely the point." Niles grinned. "We plan to loosen a flange attached to connecting steam pipes inside the vault. Then, we'll open the topside doors wide, and cover the vault over with bamboo rods, twigs and brush."

"Why in heavens would you do such a thing? The loose flange, and built up condensate, will be dangerous."

"We're going to drive the beasts toward the vault," said Niles. "The Rhino-pards will drop inside, trapped. Then our boy, here, will fire off a Very pistol. I'll remain at the facility with you, Mr. Runge, looking for the flare. Once it goes off, we'll turn the system back on-line as quickly as possible—"

"A fast start up?" Runge interrupted, shaking his head. "The steam rushing through the line will collide with trapped condensate at Vault C and cause a water-hammer. This is a most dangerous proposition."

"The beasts have thick hides, making them almost impervious to bullets," Niles explained, nodding kindly. "The water-hammer will explode at the loose flange, and scorch them with hot steam flooding the vault."

Runge stood before them with an odd smirk on his face. The countenance didn't reveal whether the Plant Operator thought their plan foolhardy, or ingenious. Maybe he didn't appreciate the prospect of the steam line being damaged by the plan.

Then, Runge crossed his arms and stared at Niles deprecatingly.

Niles must have been thinking the same as Kevin. "We anticipate the only damage to the steam line would occur within the vault. The piping in Vault C will have to be reworked, but that would only take the system off-line for a couple of days."

"Thankfully," said Cunningham, "it's only early fall."

"You could just use a Rocket-Powered Recoilless Weapon," Runge replied, flashing a sardonic grin. "They were developed toward the end of the Great War."

"But they've never been put to use in the field," Cunningham retorted, stepping closer to Runge. "Blazes, the thought of using an untested weapon in an urban setting, jam-packed with civilians, is unprecedented."

"The havoc caused in the city today was likely more dreadful."

"You've heard about that?" Cunningham sounded chagrinned. "Most unpleasant business, most unpleasant indeed."

"Have you thought about evacuating part of the city?" Runge inquired.

"There just isn't time," Niles pled. "We need to implement this plan, or more people are going to get killed and maimed."

Runge glanced upward at the clock mechanism mounted in the center of the wall. A smile crept across his face. It seemed as though he'd begun warming up to the idea; his facility would be instrumental in bringing about the demise of the beasts.

"Very well, then." Runge beamed at the hunters. "I'm at your service."

"Great to have you aboard!" Cunningham said, shaking Runge's hand.

As the moment passed, Kevin was drawn to the immense clockwork in the center of the room. He watched the intricate cogs turn and interplay with precision. Runge shuffled a little closer. The Plant Operator rubbed his hands together, interested in an intellectual conundrum. His eyes widened.

"Tell me, lad," Runge whispered. "What intrigues you so?"

Kevin shrugged. "This clockwork stands three stories high. It seems rather overbuilt for the purposes that you've described."

"The entire universe runs on clockwork," Runge snickered.

Kevin glanced at the Plant Operator blankly. He pondered his situation and wondered what powers Runge had over time and space, the cosmos. There seemed to be something deliberate that brought Kevin to this world, something beyond mere chance and happenstance.

Niles turned to Kevin, snapping him from deep thought. "Remember once you have the beasts trapped, you fire off the Very pistol. Leave the rest to me and Mr. Runge."

"Got it right here," Kevin said. He patted the flare gun, snug in a shoulder holster.

"Then we're ready to shove off!" Cunningham bellowed. "And face the peril that awaits us."

CHAPTER SEVENTEEN

Sarah got behind the wheel again and drove them across town. They stopped at the quarters to retrieve rifles and equipment, and then headed to the common. By the time they arrived at the public park, the day had settled into evening dusk. A shimmer of reddish orange caught in the clouds from the setting sun.

She felt the brisk air as she alighted from the Rover. The clouds would block out moonlight, making it harder to see during the hunt.

Tightening up his leather jacket, Kevin ran a hand through his purple hair, and then began checking over the equipment like a professional.

Cunningham glanced at him curiously. "Wearing that thing again?"

"Just figured that if I die today, it would be better to check out wearing my favorite jacket."

The Great Hunter nodded with a gentle smile.

Sarah grinned, but Kevin didn't seem to notice her approval of his outfit. He was absorbed in getting ready for the excursion.

Kevin tucked the Ray-gun into a holster that Cunningham had devised. Then, he checked over the Very pistol, loading a flare. It clicked open like a shotgun, receiving the flare in a tubular chamber. The handle was polished mahogany, but the rest of it was brass, including the hammer.

Finally, he examined both rifles, making sure the barrels were clear, and the weapons fully loaded. Then he checked to make sure the safeties were flipped on.

Cunningham stepped over and reached for the Weatherby. He stood dressed in his hunting clothes with the bush hat tilted back on his large pate. Looking Kevin over thoughtfully, he stepped closer. "Are you sure that you're up to this, lad?"

"Ready as I'll ever be," Kevin replied.

"That's not quite what I'm asking," he whispered. "I mean, are you up to it?"

"He's perfectly capable," Sarah chimed in. "We both are, actually."

Cunningham pulled a face, taken aback that she'd heard him. His eyebrows shot up, and he stumbled. They both looked Sarah over in amazement. She wore her Victorian dress pinned up so that the fabric didn't catch on the ground. She had traded her laced-up high heels for a pair of rubber Wellington boots.

The change in footwear was understandable. But they seemed surprised to see that she'd donned a grey shooting jacket over her dress. A large pad covered the right shoulder. Sarah registered Kevin's astonishment.

"Did you think only the boys would handle those rifles?" Sarah taunted him.

"Well, the truth of it…" Kevin stammered. "I didn't really—"

"Be careful, lad," Cunningham interjected.

"Didn't really, what?" she demanded.

"I didn't really think," Kevin muttered, "you'd find a shooting jacket in your size."

"Oh, this old thing," said Sarah, smiling proudly. "Why I've had this for some time, and had occasion to use it, but infrequently."

She stepped toward Cunningham with her hand out. He looked at her bewildered. As Sarah moved closer, he didn't seem to realize that she had reached for the Weatherby. The Great Hunter eventually registered what she demanded. "Blazes!" he hooted. "You'll not take my rifle."

"But I'll be in the thick of danger," she reasoned. "And you'll be positioned behind the barricade with the 10th Hussars."

Cunningham's eyes glimmered with disdain at the mention of him relying upon the soldiers. The hunter shook his head. He worked the bolt and checked over the weapon as though the discussion were over.

Sarah stood by, looking dismayed. Letting out a huff, Sarah turned her eyes upon Kevin and kicked at dirt. He obviously felt bad for her, and was likely concerned about her safety. Kevin faced the hunter. "She may have a point—"

"Absolutely not!" Cunningham bellowed. "Giving her a rifle could be dangerous. Why, she might shoot one of us by mistake."

Sarah crossed her arms and pouted.

"But she shouldn't be made to face the beasts defenseless."

Cunningham rubbed his chin, considering.

"I've had training with firearms," Sarah muttered.

"But in the event the Rhino-pards get through," said Cunningham, "we'll need a big bore rifle to take them down."

"She can't be left unarmed," Kevin pled.

"Not saying that," Cunningham replied. "Not saying that at all. I'm suggesting that we give her the Gibbs, and I'll hold on to the Weatherby… in case they get through."

Sarah smiled and reached for the Gibbs. Kevin handed it over without further discussion. Then, he scratched his head. "Now I'll be unarmed."

"You've got the Ray-gun," Cunningham offered. "Use that if they get too close."

"What if it doesn't work?" Kevin complained.

"Worked in the tunnel, didn't it?"

Kevin nodded.

"And besides, you could always fire the Very pistol at them." Cunningham grinned. "Let's get on with it, shall we?"

****

Darkness crept over the city like a thick blanket as they ventured into the common. Kevin had the knapsack slung over a shoulder with the lantern inside. They would need it when entering the tunnels, but he considered using it to cross the park.

Sarah lugged the Gibbs at port arms. She had rounds shoved into holders on her shooting jacket. Beside her, Cunningham resembled a bandito with bandoliers of rounds slung crisscrossed over his chest, and the Weatherby tucked into the nook of his left arm.

"You don't seem burdened at all," Kevin said to Sarah.

She glanced at him puzzled. "Why should I be burdened?"

"Just… you know," Kevin replied sheepishly. "Carrying the rifle and all."

"This rifle here," she said, holding it up with minimal effort.

Sarah truly seemed baffled by his comments. The insinuation that she hailed from a weaker sex was lost on her. The two rifles had taxed him quickly during the tracking party. Kevin expected that she would feel laden by the Gibbs, but she didn't show any sign of slowing down.

He contemplated his experiences in this bizarre new world. Although women were formally clad in Victorian attire, they held equal positions to men, facing danger and physical toils the same as their male counterparts. Kevin's world was only beginning to understand that women were as capable as men. Niles and Cunningham hadn't really hesitated in adding her to the team.

"Carrying two of the rifles had proven to be burdensome," Kevin tried to explain. "So, I figured the Gibbs might weigh you down a bit, is all."

"Well, I certainly am not lugging two rifles around," she quipped.

"Enough, now," Cunningham snapped. "There's no time for this petty bickering."

"Yes, sir," Kevin replied.

"And you toughen up," Cunningham said, pointing at Kevin.

When they stepped onto the grassy plain, the park bustled with the activities being directed by the Royal Engineers. Gas lanterns illuminated the area. A large steam vault had been thrust open. The steel doors were removed by workers and taken away. The concrete vault had piping running throughout. It resembled a small basement filled with pipes, levers, and gauges.

An industrial mechanic worked at loosening a flange with a large wrench. Merely an iron plate, the flange connected two sections of steam pipe together. Large bolts fastened the pipe sections to the flange. The mechanic adjusted the bolts, loosening them enough to create a weak point in the line.

The mechanic climbed a ladder affixed to the concrete box and stepped topside. This vault spanned six meters in length and three meters wide; it looked about five meters deep. The vault appeared large enough to hold a Rhino-pard, but Kevin wondered if it could trap two beasts. Partially cat-like creatures, he pictured them springing from the hold.

Workers placed bamboo rods across the opening and then piled sticks on top of them. A cedar tree had been dropped on the edge of the wood line. More workers chopped branches off the tree with hatchets. They spread the evergreen limbs over the bamboo rods and sticks, effectively concealing the vault from view.

The hunting party stood at the edge of the vault, looking over the trap. All of the camouflage hid the opening very well. But standing there perusing the mound of evergreens, Kevin wondered if the Rhino-pards would steer clear of it.

Stepping back a few paces, he looked the park over and tried to discern whether or not the trap stood out from the grassy plain. He expected it appeared like a heap, but gladly found that it blended with the rest of the greenery.

"How does it look, lad?" Cunningham called to him.

"The brush on top of the bamboo doesn't standout much. If they're running fast, the Rhino-pards aren't likely to see it."

"They won't have much of choice in going through here."

He walked back to Cunningham. The Great Hunter slapped him on the shoulder. "Things are shaping up timely," said Cunningham.

Kevin looked around. Various steam-propelled work trucks had been brought into the park. The vehicles were set in two rows. Each row started near the wood line about fifty meters apart, and then the lines of trucks got closer together as they neared the vault.

The trucks formed a passageway leading directly to the trap and continued on toward a fortified position. Sandbags were piled at the end of the rows of work trucks, running in-between the vehicles closing off a gauntlet. Behind the sandbags, the 10th Hussars were busy preparing for a conflict.

Kevin noticed a primitive-looking Bazooka being positioned behind the barricade. He figured it was the weapon that Runge had talked about. The thought of so many weapons being pointed at the wood line, a direction Kevin and Sarah would be fleeing from, caused him to gasp for air. The soldiers hustled around jovially, itching to take part in the victory.

"Tell me what's the issue, lad?" Cunningham whispered.

"These guys have me more concerned for Sarah's safety..." Kevin explained, "than the Rhino-pards that we're hunting."

Cunningham nodded, affirmatively. "I'll be behind the barricade with their captain. No shots will be fired downrange, unless I give the order."

The comment made Kevin feel a little better. Still, the thought of all the excitement had him concerned that something could go wrong. A shot could get squeezed off in haste, causing a volley of rounds to follow, directed right at them.

****

Later, after workers maneuvered the steam trucks into place, Sarah watched Cunningham, as he slung the Weatherby over his shoulder. He nodded to Sarah and gave Kevin a pat on the arm.

"These fellows are very well disciplined," he commented, heading toward the barricade. "If nothing else, they are very well disciplined, indeed."

Sarah nodded in agreement.

"I certainly hope so," Kevin replied. "But this is an unusual situation."

"Toughen up!" Cunningham jibed.

Sarah giggled at the comment directed toward her young companion. But Kevin didn't seem to find it funny, and tensed up as the Great Hunter demanded.

Cunningham's bush hat jutted up and down, bobbing as he sauntered off. "Most unusual is an understatement," he muttered, walking away. "You know what to do, lad! So, go ahead and do it well!"

Before Cunningham had gotten ten paces away from them, the soldiers were in position and the workers had cleared the field. Most everyone had already left, except for a few stragglers who were picking up tools.

Gas lanterns were cut out and the park fell into darkness. Sarah could hardly see Kevin standing beside her. Then, her eyes adjusted. Kevin reached into the knapsack for the lantern.

Patting the holsters for the Very pistol and his Ray-gun, Kevin sought reassurance from being equipped with weapons. Sarah shook her head and laughed.

He lit the lantern and held it up.

"What's so funny?" he asked.

"You, silly," she replied.

Kevin glanced at Sarah. "Are you ready?"

"Ready as I'll ever be," she answered, smiling. "Are you?"

He nodded sternly. "Let's get going then."

They turned and started walking toward the wood line. She had the Gibbs slung over her shoulder and he wore the knapsack.

A host of soldiers watching, Sarah could feel many eyes upon them. Kevin appeared self-conscious of his movements. She wondered if he was up for the task. Sarah stepped lightly upon the grass, making their departure look graceful, and her presence apparently brought him some comfort.

CHAPTER EIGHTEEN

Crossing the grassy field to the wood line only took a few minutes. Kevin paused, swinging the lantern, while searching for a path to the access tunnel. It had been easy to spot in the daylight, so he hadn't expected it to be difficult to find. Everything appeared obscured in the darkness, with tree branches and shrubs jutting all over.

"Where is the stinking path?" Kevin griped.

"How should I know?" Sarah replied. "You've been over it before. Not me."

"It was right around here," he said, motioning with the lantern. "Let's just bend down and get a better angle to spot the broken branches."

"Well, it seems to be far more difficult to locate at night."

"Tell me about it," he complained, kneeling to view the brush.

"You don't have to snap. This is merely a momentary delay."

"This little delay is not the problem," said Kevin. "We'll find the path in due time. What worries me is trying to make our way back, over such an obscure path, with the beasts chasing us."

Sarah let out a sigh. "That really wasn't much of an apology."

"Sorry, I'm just trying to focus on the task at hand." He looked at her dutifully. "My apologies for letting my manners slip."

She smiled, happily. And he was pleasantly taken by her demand for respect.

"I promise not to let it happen again," he said, wondering if he should explain his feelings. "Unless we're getting pursued by the Rhino-pards."

"That's much better." Sarah turned, pointing. "And look over there."

Kevin followed the trace of her fingertip. The Rhino-pards were far more agile than he'd realized. They left scant trace of their route.

When the lantern finally shone upon the path, it was only about half a meter wide. The brush had bent back into place whenever the beasts thundered over the pathway. Each time the beasts trod from the access pipe to the park, they carefully kept to a tight path, concealing the trail to their bedding grounds.

Sarah started toward the path. He reached out and grabbed her shoulder tightly, halting her progress. Turning, she scowled at Kevin until registering that he was merely being cautious.

"They come out at night to feed," he whispered. "We have to avoid walking into them."

Nodding in understanding, she stood by quietly while he shined the lantern into the woods. Kevin looked for movement in the shadows. He listened for the sound of a Rhino-pard stepping on the forest floor, twigs snapping and leaves crunching.

The wooded track of land remained silent. He couldn't see any sign of the beasts within the little forest. Kevin stepped down the path a short way.

He stopped and looked around. The only sound came from his own breathing. Puffy clouds of mist drifted under the lantern light. After listening a moment longer, Kevin waved for Sarah to join him.

"Now we get to serve as bait," Sarah whispered, heading down the path.

"You're the bait," he muttered nervously. "They seem to prefer women. Remember?"

"Thank you, Kevin Barnes, for that gentle reminder. Let's move along now."

"You're starting to sound like Cunningham."

"Why thank you," she replied, grinning. "He is a wonderful attribute to country and crown."

They began moving down the path. Kevin and Sarah walked carefully to avoid making noise. She held the Gibbs at port arms, ready to fire if necessary. And Kevin paid careful attention to each way the path twisted and turned. He expected their egress would be made in extreme haste.

"Do you think we should put out the lantern?" he asked. "Maybe the light will attract their attention."

"The beasts will smell us long before they hear our footsteps, or see the light."

"You have a point there," said Kevin. "But I'd prefer not to advertise our presence as much as possible."

"Advertise?" she questioned. "What has any of this to do with *advertisements*?"

"I'll tell you about it later. We need to focus on the Rhino-pards."

She huffed and continued on behind him quietly.

Kevin stepped into the mud that he'd encountered previously. He glanced at the ground and saw his own boot print in the path, except there was an enormous paw print near it. Claw marks had scraped into the moist soil, measuring sixteen centimeters wide.

Another print lay in the path a meter ahead. The sight of large prints served as an ominous reminder of how deadly the creatures were. Kevin took a deep breath, feeling the cool air enter his lungs. It was a heavy, moist gulp of air that didn't seem to deliver oxygen to his body. He felt unsettled about entering the tunnels again. Having been full of rage when he'd last charged into the tunnels, Kevin hadn't taken the time to contemplate the danger.

This time around, things felt much different. He was easing down the pathway with plenty of time to consider the foolhardy nature of this errand. Before the beasts had fled into the tunnel, and Kevin chased madly after them. He had expected to trail behind them. Somehow that felt safer. Now, Kevin knew the Rhino-pards were meandering through the catacombs, intent on emerging from the tunnels to feed. At some point, he chanced walking into them head-on.

Kevin caught a glimpse of Sarah's face in the lamplight. Her eyes had grown wide at the sight of the large prints.

"Are you all right?" he asked, locking glances.

"Everything is perfectly suitable." Sarah tightened her grip on the rifle. "Why on heavens would you ask?"

"Just making sure that you want to go through with this."

"Nothing has caused me to change my mind," Sarah replied, dismissively.

He began to wonder if this was a good idea. With all of the access points closed off, the beasts would likely head topside through the only tunnel that wasn't shut up. The Rhino-pards would emerge near the trap anyway. Kevin wondered if it was worth risking their lives.

They continued down the path in silence. The plan was merely for the two of them to enter the tunnel and provide a scent for the beasts to follow. And the scent of a female was preferred.

Once the beasts picked up their presence, they would chase the bait and barge onto the field, and then fall into the trap unaware. Niles figured if the Rhino-pards exited the tunnels on happenstance without pursuing prey, they would be more cautious and likely avert the snare.

"We have a job to do," Sarah continued. "There's no sense dwelling on danger."

"What makes you say that?" said Kevin, turning back to her.

"Why, it is written all over your face." She giggled. "You look truly concerned about this expedition."

"Really?" Kevin shook his head, then started back down the path.

"Certainly," Sarah confirmed. "You obviously question the wisdom of this effort."

"The Rhino-pards would head out of that tunnel anyway."

"Most likely," she agreed. "But they would be more cautious having encountered the closed access points. They would be more inclined to sniff out the trap if we weren't sent in to distract them."

"They are very smart," said Kevin. "I'll give you that. You're probably right, and we are in the middle of this already."

Sarah patted his shoulder. He felt comforted again, for a moment. A sinking feeling overcame him when they turned a bend in the path.

The opening to the tunnel lay before them. Kevin immediately noticed that workers had pulled the grate back slightly, and the steel pipe was partly exposed. Thinking of their retreat, he had counted on the grate slowing the Rhino-pards down before hitting the mucky path, but now he wondered if it would hold.

An eerie feeling ran through him. The lantern cast illumination over the entire opening. Kevin thought the lantern was too bright to take inside the tunnels. Rays of light would refract through the catacombs and alert the Rhino-pards to their presence. The beasts were smart and seemed to register the rifles when the hunters had stumbled upon them, as though the Rhino-pards had encountered firearms in the past.

They would surely remember the lantern as well. Kevin set the lamp down near the opening.

"What are you doing?" Sarah questioned. "We'll need the lantern to see inside the tunnel."

"It's way too bright," Kevin said, fumbling for a pocket. "That lantern will attract attention, alert them to us."

"We won't get far without any light."

Kevin pulled out his cell phone. Pleased to find it still had some juice, he turned on the light, and caught the amazed look in Sarah's eyes.

"Pray-tell, what is that gizmo, Mr. Barnes?"

"This is just a cell phone. But it has a light app."

"A cell phone? What on heavens is that?"

Kevin realized that he hadn't seen any sort of phone since he'd woken up on the steam train. Strange how this world had developed all sorts of technology, but didn't have something as basic as a phone, which had been developed in his world in the late 1800s.

"Just a gizmo, like you were saying." He shook his head. "Around here, it would be more of a toy."

Sarah smiled at his acquiescence. "A toy with a practical little light."

"That's basically the case, I'm afraid," he added.

"Why on heavens would you be *afraid* of a toy?"

Kevin shrugged. "The phone has the potential for other applications, but they can't be used right now."

"Developing technology," Sarah grinned. "How splendid."

"Shall we get on with it?" Kevin said, pointing toward the opening.

Sarah nodded affirmatively.

Kevin held the phone in one hand, and his Ray-gun in the other. Sarah unslung the Gibbs and worked the bolt to chamber a round, and then they stepped inside the dark tunnel.

CHAPTER NINETEEN

Inside, they trudged through trickling water, about twenty paces, and the scant illumination from the moonlight fell away. Kevin and Sarah plied their way through the blackest of passages.

A stench wafted through the tunnel, almost causing Kevin to regurgitate. Beyond the section of steel pipe, they walked down a brick passageway. The putrid odor grew stronger the further they delved into the tunnel.

Kevin's head began to swirl. He covered his nose and breathed through his mouth. Checking on Sarah, he found that she'd instinctively done the same.

Detritus caught along the bottom of the tunnel, sticks and clumps of muck. Kevin stumbled a few times. He found the little flashlight helped detect larger heaps of debris, but smaller mounds lay hidden in the shadows.

The plan of maneuvering through the tunnels, with Rhino-pards chasing after them, daunted his spirits, but thoughts of tripping on debris alarmed him even more. Dread slipped over Kevin like a heavy blanket, smothering his breath, and trapping him in a paralysis. He found himself pausing at a small clump of sticks and muck, unable to move.

Sarah elbowed him. "Let's get going. The obstacle's not that big."

"Sure thing," Kevin said, stepping forward reluctantly.

"This definitely is a stinky tunnel. Makes one anxious to get on with it."

Then, Kevin felt his foot squish into something dense. He pointed the light down. Part of a women's torso lay on the deck, cleaved away at the waist, an arm torn off, and the head missing. Kevin felt air rush from his lungs. Her dress, saturated in grimy water, had dark crimson stains, discernible in the wavering light.

Sarah cupped a hand over her mouth. Kevin stepped away from the corpse, registering fear in her eyes. The sight of a slain person decomposing in the dank tunnel sobered him. It pushed heroic bravura to the side; the reality of carnage and death sent a shudder down his spine. Now survival instincts kicked into gear. Adrenaline pumped up his spine.

Further ahead, they came upon the intersecting tunnels where Kevin had last encountered a Rhino-pard. He stopped and listened carefully. Nothing. Not a sound. Expecting to hear water thrashing or the snort from a beast, Kevin found the absolute stillness unsettling. *Perhaps one of them lay in the darkness ready to pounce*, he worried.

He held the Ray-gun ready to fire. Sarah picked up on his lead and shouldered the Gibbs. Then she stepped against the tunnel wall, ready to fire a clear shot past Kevin. This impressed him. Kevin had admired her gumption, but hadn't given her enough credit for understanding tactical maneuvers in the field. He'd worried about potentially being shot by friendly fire.

Stepping forward, he held the light to the side, giving the impression they were to the left of the tunnel, while Sarah pressed against the right side and Kevin walked down the center. He knew the effort was futile. When the Rhino-pards charged, anyone not keeping ahead of them would be trampled.

Kevin slowly stepped into the cross-tunnels. He anxiously looked left and right, trying to determine if the creatures were down either passageway.

The tunnels were extremely dark. He couldn't see beyond three meters, and what little he could discern, appeared obscured in the miniscule light. Kevin pocketed the cell phone and tried to adjust his eyes to the darkness.

He couldn't see a thing. Everything was pitch-black; and no matter how hard he tried adjusting his eyes, Kevin couldn't see anything. Utter blackness.

So, he paused to listen for the beasts.

The only thing he heard was Sarah breathing. As he focused on his sense of hearing, Kevin became more acute to her heartbeat and intense breathing.

"Kevin, what are you doing?" she finally asked.

He didn't want to respond. Now wasn't the time for talking, but she sounded annoyed and would likely ask again, only louder. "Give me a moment."

"A moment for what?" said Sarah.

"For listening. Try to hold your breath, please."

He heard her take a gulp. Everything became silent, except for his own heartbeat. The pounding seemed unusually loud. Fear. Anxiety. Kevin focused intently.

No other sounds.

He listened for thrashing.

Nothing.

The Rhino-pards couldn't be nearby.

Kevin relaxed a bit. He grew consumed with the conundrum of which tunnel to choose. He pulled out the light. Remembering how Cunningham had tracked the beasts, he glanced at the corners of each tunnel.

There were scraps of skin on each one. The Rhino-pards had used these intersecting tunnels as a major throughway. It was difficult to determine which way to go. Glancing at Sarah, she shrugged, seeming as confused as him.

Then, her mouth went agape. She pointed. Kevin's heart palpitated with panic. *A Rhino-pard lingered in the shadows*, he thought.

Turning, he didn't see anything beyond the light. The water at their feet remained still. Nothing charged them; Kevin took a deep breath. His elevated heart rate quickly subsided. Sarah pointed down low on the wall.

Kevin knelt and inspected the brick near the tunnel on the right. On the corner, he noticed a dense collection of Rhino-pard hide that had scuffed the craggy surface. Obviously, one of the beasts was shorter and stockier than the other. They had ventured to the right more than any other direction.

"This way," he said, turning right.

"Indeed." She grinned proudly. "Apparently, we're in pursuit."

"Just remember to turn left, when we come back this way."

"I'll be on your heels the entire way."

He took a deep breath, considering their plight. Two fearless beasts would chase them, infuriated by weapons that harmed the creatures, but couldn't drop them. The Rhino-pards would charge madly.

Although the beam of light only cast a short distance, the water and damp brick reflected its glow down a long passageway. The tunnel appeared to stretch indefinitely. Kevin couldn't see any side tunnels ahead.

The open tunnel ahead of them gave him some comfort. He might see the creatures from a distance, giving the trackers a head start when fleeing. But then he worried the long tunnel gave the Rhino-pards a chance to build up momentum. Twists and turns provided a human advantage. Now, he wished for intersecting tunnels as a means to elude the beasts.

Kevin paused. He began to consider turning back. They merely had to enter the tunnels to leave a scent. The Rhino-pards would likely head this way. Perhaps they had done enough, he surmised.

Sarah nudged him from behind, prodding him along.

They hadn't gone far enough and he knew it. She knew it, too. Kevin figured if they reached the next intersection, wherever it was located, then the scent could be fanned in a few directions. Then they could turn back.

They trudged forward. Water grew deeper and deeper the further they traveled down the tunnel. The grimy water soaked through his boots. Retreat would be difficult. This was beginning to feel like a suicide mission.

The length of the open tunnel alone was daunting. It seemed to extend forever without an intersection or a turn.

A glimmer of reflecting light revealed a tunnel to the left. The narrow passageway had been indiscernible until they were directly upon it. Kevin stopped abruptly to inspect it. Sarah collided into him. She shoved him forward by her delayed reaction. The beating of his heart quickened.

The side tunnel was narrower than the others. A Rhino-pard would have to squeeze to get into it. The corners didn't reveal any scrapes of hide.

Kevin shook his head. "Nothing down there."

They continued on another twenty paces and found a passageway to the right. It seemed to be narrow like the last one.

As Kevin flashed the light to inspect the corners of the tunnel, a thrashing emitted from the murky waters.

The sound was less than five meters away.

He wanted to bolt.

Another flutter in the water.

This noise didn't suggest a large animal. Kevin shined the light down the passageway. A large duck shook its wings, apparently injured. Glancing back to Sarah, he smiled and let out a sigh of relief.

Then, a glow of cat-like eyes shone further down the tunnel.

"Run!" Kevin yelled, raising the Ray-gun.

The beast pounced.

He fired just below the menacing eyes. A howl of pain, but it kept coming. Kevin fired two more times. Striking the creature at least once, it slowed the pursuit.

Water rose around Kevin's legs in waves as the Rhino-pard closed the distance. He stood solid, grasping the light and the Ray-gun. Kevin fired three times into its right shoulder.

The beast wailed.

Kevin turned and ran hard.

The dank water slowed him down.

He could feel the Rhino-pard snorting. It grew near enough to strike soon. Kevin's throat went dry with panic. Another set of pounding feet echoed through the catacombs. The other Rhino-pard had joined in the chase.

Kevin saw Sarah plodding along. He closed in on her as the beasts prepared to take him down. She had trouble running through the boot-high water.

Sarah fled down the tunnel just a meter in front of him.

The lead Rhino-pard trailed only two meters behind Kevin, with the companion beast on its tail. If Sarah tripped, they would both get trampled, and torn to shreds.

Kevin's lungs burned and legs felt like lead. His pulse raced with dread. They weren't going to make it back to the access point. No way.

A surge of adrenaline, and Kevin pushed forward.

Grabbing onto Sarah's shoulder, he jerked her into the narrow side-passageway and dove in beside her. They both landed in the filthy water, cell phone cracking on the brick. A flicker of light still illuminated the catacombs from the gadget.

The Rhino-pards charged past the tunnel entrance.

Kevin and Sarah clambered from the murky water. He glanced into darkness and feared the tunnel a dead end.

Gathering their bearings, Kevin heard the beasts circle back. The stout Rhino-pard had been in the rear, but now nosed into the side tunnel. Kevin and Sarah stepped back while facing the brute.

They raised their weapons.

The other creature rose on its hind legs, placing both paws on the other's rump. Claws flexed into the hide of its companion. A ring of crimson circled its maw.

Pushing into the narrow tunnel, the hefty beast shouldered into the passageway, hide scraping on brick, then it got caught up on the small opening.

Forward progress impeded, the stout Rhino-pard let out a roar. Long fangs whipped saliva; the shrill pierced Kevin's ears, and he felt the heat of the beast's breath.

The Rhino-pard's yellow eyes shined menacingly in the darkness. When the creature reached a standstill, it blinked, intelligently, registering the pursuit had stymied. Its companion bounced and kicked in the main passageway, seeming anxious to push through.

Protected by the narrow passageway, Kevin and Sarah eased away. She slung the rifle over her shoulder without firing a shot. Kevin fumbled with the cell phone and the light went out. The tunnel became pitch-black.

Everything turned silent, except the heavy breathing from the Rhino-pards, and Kevin's racing heart.

Kevin turned to Sarah.

Grabbing her arm, they plied their way into the darkness, fearing the tunnel led nowhere.

CHAPTER TWENTY

They stumbled along the narrow tunnel, trying to put distance between themselves and the beasts. Sarah heard the angry Rhino-pards in the distance, pounding at the passageway, and then finally stampeding off.

Reaching into a pocket, Kevin pulled out his gadget, and checked to see how much juice was left. The screen was cracked and water dripped from the casing. His phone had about twenty percent power left. He told her it would die within twenty minutes, at best, given the damage. Sarah wrapped her arm around his, but still managed to stumble in the darkness.

He flicked on the light. It worked.

They steadied their footing and pressed onward.

She had expected the small side tunnel to either run into a dead end, or quickly lead into a major passageway. But the tunnel continued on endlessly.

"Do you think this will take us to access the surface?" Sarah asked.

"This has got to connect somewhere," Kevin replied. "Just not sure if it will get us back to the way we came in."

"We need to get out safely," said Sarah.

"The other access points are sealed off," Kevin said. "I think we ventured too far when trying to leave a scent. We should have turned back sooner."

"Too late for that now."

"Just wish that I'd stopped us… before we got to the beasts."

"Nothing you can do about it."

Kevin looked at the power level again. Still reading twenty percent, but he suspected it would drop lower soon given his comments. "Come on," he said. "We've got to get a move on."

"What's the matter?" she wondered aloud.

"The battery for this light is running down. And we need to get clear before they circle around on us."

"Doesn't that contraption of yours work properly?"

"This thing is meant for another place and time."

"Afraid that I don't quite follow." He often confused her.

"Never mind," he said. "We've got to move along."

Kevin picked up his stride anxiously, slogging through the dank water. Sarah pressed on beside him, not losing pace for a moment.

They made a lot of noise, and the beasts likely heard them, while meandering through the catacombs in hot pursuit. She wondered if they'd make it out alive.

****

Eventually, the tunnel intersected with a major passageway. They came to a halt and Kevin scanned the small beam of light along the brick.

"Thank heavens we finally reached another tunnel," said Sarah.

Kevin smiled, also relieved.

"Why, I began to worry that passageway would never end," Sarah said. "Just terrified it would simply dead end." Nothing had shown on her countenance reflecting fear. She was truly unassailable.

"Me too," Kevin muttered. He felt embarrassed that she had more fortitude. Turning the light back to the catacombs, she caught him glancing at her.

"What are you looking at?" Sarah quipped. "Thought we had to move along."

"Sure, we've got to get out of here," he said, chagrinned.

"Which way do we go?"

Kevin scanned the small beam and saw markings etched into the brick. *Cunningham.* "This way," he said, turning left.

"How can you be sure?"

"Cunningham marked the way," he said, pointing.

"The Great Hunter," she giggled. "Blazes!"

Kevin shook his head. He couldn't understand how she faced the grave predicament so lightheartedly. Then, he wondered if she fully appreciated the gravity of the situation, or perhaps in her world, life and death situations occurred far more frequently.

He picked up his pace to a trot. The murky water became shallow as they pressed forward. Kevin felt less resistance on his jackboots; he moved more quickly as he ran. Sarah plodded a step behind, her Wellington boots sloshing through the water.

Another intersection lay ahead. Kevin didn't even pause, remembering clearly the path they had taken during the tracking party.

They branched off and kept moving.

"Are you sure we're headed in the right direction?" said Sarah.

"Positive."

He glanced down at the cell phone. The power level had dropped, depicting a red battery. Kevin's lungs started to burn and his legs ached from the effort and dampness. Easing his gait, he tried to level off and recover a little.

"Why are you slowing down?" This from Sarah who didn't sound the least bit winded. "Let's move along faster."

"Need to conserve our strength for the escape…" he gasped for breath, "from the beasts chasing us."

"If we push on now, we might not run into them again."

She had a point, but somehow he figured the Rhino-pards were too smart to let them waltz out of there. And the beasts knew the tunnel system well. "They're going to try and beat us to the access point."

"How could those animals possibly think ahead like that?" Sarah said.

"Can't explain it," Kevin replied. "Just have a feeling in my gut."

Sarah's shadow reflected on the grimy brick wall, head shaking. He knew she wanted to sprint ahead of the beasts and make a dash for the common. The creatures were smart. And the Rhino-pards had acute senses. The beasts could likely hear the slogging footfalls echo through the tunnels, giving away their flight.

Such powerful and agile creatures could bound through the main passageway, and then lay in wait like giant cats on a grassy plain, biding their time for the prey to come to them. Kevin expected that no matter how fast they ran, the Rhino-pards would be ahead of them, waiting for the kill.

"Let's conserve our energy," he said. "Just in case we have to fight them."

Sarah glanced at him through the dim light. A look of dire concern cast upon her face, reflecting a dissipating hope of evading the beasts. Her pace slowed, and then she stopped advancing altogether.

"What is it?" Kevin called back to her.

She didn't respond.

He stopped.

Then, he heard the bolt of the Gibbs clanking a round into the chamber. "What are you doing?" he asked, knowing she'd checked the load.

"Preparing for the fight," Sarah said, stepping towards him. She held the large rifle ready to fire, with the butt lodged into her shoulder.

"We haven't much time left with this light."

"At some point, we are going to run right into them."

Sarah had finally spoken what he'd been thinking for some time. The splashing through the water would alert the beasts to their approach, and the commotion served to obscure the Rhino-pards in the dark, quiet tunnel.

Nothing would give away the beasts, not their breathing or stench.

Kevin and Sarah would run into the creatures and get mauled. She was right. Slowing down and preparing for a conflict was the best option. He still feared losing their light, getting trapped in the maze of dark tunnels.

"You're right," Kevin finally said. "Let's prepare to fight, and keep the pace as fast as we can move without making too much noise."

"And keep that light pointed down," she added.

Reaching an intersection, Kevin paused, trying to remember which way led out. He recalled stopping there before, but Cunningham hadn't marked the path. This was near where the tracking party had encountered the beasts for the first time.

The ceiling suddenly felt low and the walls seemed to be closing in. Kevin's heart raced. Anxiety pulsated through him. The pressure of making the right decision caused him to panic. Fear of a mistake fogged his brain.

Frantic.

He was running out of time.

Every second counted.

Power to the phone was winding down, so they couldn't afford to make a mistake. Time ticked, almost accelerated by his paralysis.

"This way," he finally said, pointing.

"Are you sure?"

"No," Kevin replied, "but we've got to keep moving."

Fifty paces down the tunnel, Kevin knew they'd made the right choice. "This is the right way," he whispered.

Anxiety slipped away due to the relief he felt. He took a deep breath, and then heard a splash in front of them. A heavy thud. Followed by another.

Light cast onto giant claws spread in the water before them.

Kevin reflectively ran the beam up. It caught on the creature's face. The Rhino-pard blinked its yellow eyes, then roared. The great horn shook in the shimmering light.

The Gibbs leveled alongside Kevin's right ear, and the barrel nosed ahead. The beast pounced, and the big bore rifle fired: KABOOM!

The beast wailed, but kept coming.

Kevin stepped aside.

KABOOM!!

The Rhino-pard stumbled. Sarah had remembered to shoot for the shoulder. Kevin saw a greenish fluid drip from the wound. It was the same shoulder that had already taken fire. The creature pounced again, staggered, and then limped trying to recover.

"Get back!" Kevin yelled.

Sarah tread away, her Wellie's splashing the murky water.

The beast shook off the wound, eyeing Kevin, as it slowly advanced. Behind the Rhino-pard, the tunnel lay empty.

Everything appeared blurry as shock and panic consumed him. The beast inched closer, then lost its footing. An immense rhino hind end collided with the brick wall, crushing masonry. Dust and grime fell from the ceiling.

Kevin steadied himself, clutching the Ray-gun ready to fire.

The Rhino-pard stumbled and then whipped its head. A fang tore open Kevin's sleeve, and severed his flesh. He lost his balance; the Ray-gun tumbled to the concrete floor with a splash.

He saw it lying in the standing water a meter away. The beast stabilized, poised for another attack, its mouth still smeared in blood.

Kevin retreated just as the Rhino-pard attacked.

Claws extended, baring its fangs, the beast rose on its husky hind legs, and lunged forward.

A paw swiped Kevin's chest. Sharp claws caught his jacket, cleaving through leather and meat. The blow hurled Kevin to the deck, clutching the cell phone.

The Rhino-pard slowly nosed closer.

Light cast toward a brick wall from the mobile. The beast lingered in the darkness as Kevin crawled, desperately back-peddling away. Its yellow eyes twinkled in the dark tunnel.

Another shot from the Gibbs rang out through the catacombs.

Kevin watched the eyes glowing in darkness.

The beast didn't seem injured from the shot. Its yellow portals continued moving closer, slinking toward its prey.

KABOOM!

Still, no impact on the Rhino-pard.

Then Kevin realized the shots were directed away from him. The other beast had closed in on Sarah!

He scrambled from the encroaching Rhino-pard.

Trying to rise while back-peddling, crab-like, Kevin's boot slipped in the mire. He dropped onto his rear. The cat seemed to register his vulnerability and pounced. Yellow eyes floated through the darkness.

Descending upon him, the beast poised for destruction. Claws extended and fangs dripping saliva, the beast had a thirst for death.

He kicked madly, moving out of the creature's path.

KABOOM!

The Gibbs fired again in the other direction.

Kevin wondered how long Sarah could hold out. And his own fate was imminent. He shifted right, and banged his hand into something. *The Ray-gun.*

Picking up the weapon, he began pulling the trigger before taking aim. Beams of red light traced through the air, slicing into the Rhino-pard's gut, scorching the thinner underbelly hide. It shrieked and wailed in agony.

The Rhino-pard landed, a front leg crashing into Kevin's thigh. Pain jolted through his right leg. The beast writhed upon the floor, balling up, floundering from its wounds. Then, it let out a few kicks and stopped moving altogether.

Kevin turned onto his stomach and saw yellow eyes down the tunnel. "Sarah!" he yelled. "Get down!"

A loud splash.

Kevin fired the Ray-gun in bursts.

Red beams of light shot through the dark passageway.

The stout Rhino-pard let out a wail.

Kevin noticed it backing away, the yellow eyes grew smaller. Then Sarah rushed to his side, helping Kevin clamber to his feet.

"That was close," Kevin said.

"Come, we must be quick," Sarah commanded.

They ambled past the fallen Rhino-pard. The thrashing had settled, but its menacing eyes watched them. A taste for vengeance emanated from its orbs.

Twenty paces down the tunnel, Kevin heard the beast rising. Water dribbled off of its back, cascading into the murky puddles, as large paws sloshed, moving erratically, slouching toward its prey.

A stumble. The Rhino-pard cracked into a wall; the tunnel trembled.

"Let's move!" Kevin yelled.

More sounds of the Rhino-pard staggering in the dank water, trying to steady itself. Then silence, as though it achieved its bearings.

"They'll be upon us soon," said Sarah.

Kevin picked up his pace, lungs burning and legs growing rubbery. The demands of tracking through the flooded passageways and fending off panic were taking a toll. Sarah pressed from behind, not breathing hard, seeming strong.

"The other creature will head in another direction," Sarah said. "We have to reach the intersecting tunnel before it does."

"Hope we can do it," Kevin panted.

They reached another passageway, but Kevin knew to steer toward the left. Venturing into a larger tunnel, he sensed they were nearing the access point. Kevin glanced over his shoulder, searching for the stout Rhino-pard.

"Move it!" Sarah commanded.

"Just checking to see if it's sneaking up from behind."

"You're slowing us down. Get a move on."

Kevin straightened out and pushed ahead. "Sorry," he said.

"Those things won't approach by stealth now," said Sarah. "You can rest assured."

Around a bend, Kevin saw a shimmer of light. "We're almost there," he said, feeling elated.

Then, the unmistakable sound of a Rhino-pard bounding through the passageway caught his attention. Thunderous paws pounded through the tunnel, inciting dread. Panic.

Kevin worked his legs faster, and Sarah matched him every step of the way.

CHAPTER TWENTY-ONE

Sarah breathed through her nose, trying to conserve her wind. They narrowed the distance to their egress point, as the beast closed in. She marked their progress against the pursuit of the Rhino-pard by the sound of thumping feet. She expected they'd reach the end of the tunnel before the creature got them.

Stomping from behind grew louder. The beast moved in quickly; its footfalls echoed through the catacombs.

For a moment, Sarah thought she heard two sets of paws, but wrote off the noise as reverberations. The mouth of the pipe stood less than fifty meters away. Moonlight and lampposts in the common caused light to refract into the passageway.

"We'll need to slow up..." she said, "to squeeze through the grate."

"The creature will be upon us by then. Speed up."

Sarah pumped her arms and churned her legs, pushing forward, expecting any misstep would result in a mauling.

By the time they were ten meters from the grate, the beast had closed the distance. Kevin stepped aside and grabbed Sarah's shoulder, directing her through the gap between the steel pipe and metal grate.

Then, he turned and faced the charging beast.

She paused to watch him. Kevin raised the Ray-gun as the Rhino-pard lunged into the air. Squeezing the brass trigger, beams of red light cut through the darkness. Yellow eyes bulged as the beast let out a roar of pain, misery, and wrath.

The laser blasts cut into the creature's underbelly, burning striations that bled greenish phlegm.

Sarah dashed from the opening. Kevin shimmied through the grate, and followed after her.

CHAPTER TWENTY-TWO

Outside the tunnel, Kevin saw Sarah well down the pathway. He ran after her, but glanced back toward the passageway. Through the grate, he saw the Rhino-pard writhing on the ground, balled up, front paws clawing at its chest.

Pounding emanated from the caverns.

"Run!" he screamed, picking up his pace to a mad dash.

Sarah stumbled, caught her balance, righted herself, and then kept pressing forward. Fear drove Kevin ahead. He stretched out his strides and felt surefooted, taking smooth deep breaths. Soon, he was on her heels.

A massive bang let out behind them, followed by loud clanging. The grate had broken loose. Metal shaking and clamor accompanied an angry snort.

Heavy thuds pounded the ground.

The beast was upon them.

"Faster!" Kevin called out.

Sarah picked up her pace. Wellington boots sloshed through the rivulet, as she plied through the wooded grove.

The Rhino-pard trailed in heated pursuit. Kevin marked its encroachment, faster than before, fueled by anger, pain and revenge.

Another set of paws thumped in the distance.

"Toss your rifle," Kevin called to Sarah.

She hesitated.

"I've got your back with the laser gun."

The Gibbs slipped from her hands, stock banging into a rock and then awkwardly fell over.

Kevin skipped over the gun, a foot slipping on the barrel.

Sarah pulled ahead.

The open common lay just ahead.

Kevin slowed and the beast closed in quickly. He turned and fired the Ray-gun. The laser beam cut wildly into the brush. Kevin bounced off a tree, stumbling, breaking small branches. The stout Rhino-pard moved in closer.

The larger beast picked up steam. It seemed hungry for a kill. Wild. A taste for human blood.

Stepping back onto the path, Kevin fired a lucky shot. The ray beam zapped into the creature's shoulder. The Rhino-pard lost its gait. Kevin bolted into a full sprint. He pumped his arms and felt his heart throbbing. His lungs burned.

He widened the gap. The pounding paws stampeded behind him; Kevin figured this was the final dash. *Do or die.*

The open common lay just ahead. Sarah bolted onto the grassy plain with Kevin on her heels. They ran toward the trap. Sarah cut to the right and Kevin went left, treading along the edges of the vault, spreading their scent.

A barricade lay a hundred meters ahead. The 10th Royal Hussars and Cunningham were at the ready.

The Rhino-pards cleared the wood line. Kevin heard the stomping as heavy paws pounded the earth of the immense park. Snarling and panting seemed to crawl up his neck. He had worried the creatures would sense the trap and make a break for it. Now, Kevin panicked, thinking the beasts were so bloodthirsty that they'd precisely follow the trail of their prey, missing the trap altogether.

Kevin pictured himself and Sarah being taken down just beyond the trap, out in the open field, being mauled while the Hussars fired in futility.

Both Rhino-pards had tracked after Kevin. He'd menaced them with the Ray-gun, and so the mad pursuit was directed solely at him.

He stepped closer to the edge, and then plunged into the trap.

A volley of rifle fire erupted from the barricade.

The Rhino-pards followed suit.

Kevin fell through the coverings and dropped into the vault. The scattered debris used to camouflage the trap helped break his fall, but still Kevin landed on the concrete floor; jolting pain shot through both his shins, most likely stress fractures.

He glanced up and saw the beasts crashing through the coverings. The stout Rhino-pard dropped through the brush, its front legs buckling from the fall. Then the other creature toppled into the vault, landing on the back of its companion. The stout beast wailed in pain.

Kevin reached for the Very pistol and fired a flare into the sky.

He hoped Niles would spot the fireworks before the beasts turned their attention toward ripping him to pieces.

Then, Kevin heard gurgling in the pipes. An ominous sound, even the Rhino-pards became still, trying to deduce their situation. He took the pause to assess his situation. Kevin saw a steel ladder bolted to the side of the vault.

He made a quick step for the ladder. A claw swiped across his shoulder, tearing open the leather jacket, cleaving flesh. Kevin didn't feel pain. He just pressed for the ladder, scurrying up, hoping beyond hope that the beasts wouldn't pull him back in.

His head cleared the surface. Kevin could see the 10th Hussars advancing toward the vault. Clambering out, he felt fangs sink into a jackboot. But the hold wasn't secure; he yanked the boot loose.

As Kevin clambered from the pit, he sensed the Rhino-pard had clenched a rung, along with his foot. The gurgling intensified into a rush of water being hammered through the pipeline.

He began to roll away from the opening, when the water-hammer pounded into the loosened flange. Just as the steam pipe exploded, dousing the vault with scalding hot water and steam, the agile Rhino-pard bounded off the back of the stout beast and leapt from the hole.

The stout Rhino-pard howled in agony. Its companion trampled past Kevin toward the line of vehicles. Another volley of rifle fire rang out, but the beast kept going. Steam hissed from the broken pipes.

Then, a heavy thud echoed from the hole.

Kevin glanced down and saw the beast writhe on the concrete floor of the vault. The thick hide percolated with blisters; dark skin had turned reddish, boiled from the steam. Parts of it had burned white. A tormented moan escaped its dying mouth.

The other Rhino-pard charged into a parked delivery truck, knocking it aside like a bale of hay. Steam pipes clanged onto the withered grass, and a front tire spun. Downfield, the 10th Hussars rushed after the beast, but it broke into a full trot and spread the distance between them. Among the throng, Kevin noticed a portly man wearing a pith helmet. Cunningham! He'd split from the pack, headed toward the Rover, the Weatherby cradled in his arms.

Sarah lay on the grass, mid-way to the barricade. A few soldiers had rushed to her aid, missing out on the action. Another volley of rifle fire and the beast was out of range.

Kevin met Sarah's eyes momentarily. She nodded.

He ran after the Great Hunter. Pain pulsated through both shins with each step. Racing toward the Rover, a surge of adrenaline overcame him. Soon, he caught up to Cunningham. The hunter trundled toward the vehicle, focused on every step.

Only when Kevin passed in front of him, did Cunningham seem to register the young tracker. A disconcerted look emanated from the hunter's bulging eyes.

"Blazes!" Cunningham roared. "I thought you were dead."

"Thanks for running to my aid," Kevin replied.

The Great Hunter grinned. "Let's not let this one get away."

"I'll drive," Kevin said, climbing into the Rover.

Cunningham clambered into the passenger seat as Kevin fired up the engine. The stove knocked and steam pipes rattled. He looked over at Cunningham expectantly.

"We can't wait for her to warm up," Cunningham said. "On with the chase!"

Kevin stepped on the gas and tore over the common, sending clods of dirt and grass into the air. The Rhino-pard charged over the grassy plain and cut into the shadows of a wood line. But instead of chasing after the beast, Kevin cut the wheel and headed for Tremont Street.

"What in Blazes are you doing?" Cunningham barked.

"Beating it to the point," Kevin chuckled.

"You've done lost the trail," Cunningham griped.

CHAPTER TWENTY-THREE

The Rover bounced down the cobblestone roadway, swerving in-between Hansom Cabs and steam buggies. As they crested a hill, the staunch rear end of the Rhino-pard came into view.

Cunningham shook his head. "Well I'll be," he muttered.

Kevin grinned and accelerated. The Rover hit a depression in the road, and then shot into the air. The front tires landed with a bang. He felt the vehicle suddenly swerve to the left. Fighting the wheel for control, Kevin jolted the Rover in the opposite direction. Now, it was speeding for the granite curb.

"We've had it for sure!" Cunningham bellowed.

"Nope." Kevin grinned coolly.

Cunningham's eyes widened.

Kevin fought the wheel again. The Rover shot to the left again. He did the same maneuver and it bolted right. This time, the torque had waned. After a few more corrections, the vehicle was under control.

"Heavens," said Cunningham. "Are you trying to kill us, lad?"

They cruised downhill toward the theater district. Just as Kevin shifted to higher gear, the Rhino-pard bolted left down a side street.

He braked hard, cutting the wheel. The Rover leaned, almost tipping over, while Cunningham clutched the safety bar. Momentum teetered the Rover onto two wheels.

"We're going over!" Cunningham yelped.

Kevin grinned, shaking his head.

The Rover rounded the turn, and dropped back onto all four wheels. He picked up the pursuit without losing a beat. Mashing the gas pedal, Kevin sped the Rover up, lunging over bumpy roads. They crested a hill, sending the vehicle into flight.

When the Rover landed, they jostled about the compartment. It continued traveling straight without veering.

"Blazes!" Cunningham adjusted his pith helmet.

"The creature is giving us a run for its money," Kevin said.

"I'll say…" Cunningham agreed. "Where in heavens did you learn to drive?"

"New Hampshire. Not much to do, but race around country roads."

"I'll say," said Cunningham. "Fine colony. Fine colony indeed."

"I think it's headed toward the harbor."

Cunningham seemed to be checking the safety on his Weatherby. "What makes you say that?" he muttered, finally looking up from the rifle.

"Just a hunch."

"Great hunters don't rely on hunches, son."

Then, the Rhino-pard cut down a narrow street on the right. Kevin braked hard, pushing the pedal to the floor. The Rover's front end nosed toward the ground, as the rear lunged upward. He couldn't make the turn.

Bringing the Rover to a stop, just past the side street, they surged forward, and then the back end dropped with a clang. Kevin shifted into reverse and accelerated.

Cunningham looked dumbfounded at the speed they traveled backward. Kevin merely glanced in the rearview mirrors for guidance.

He shifted into drive and turned down the side road, stepping on the gas, while scanning for the beast. It charged along at a full trot without any sign of slowing down.

Occasionally, the Rhino-pard came upon an unsuspecting pedestrian taken by surprise. The beast merely lowered its head, and horned the person to a side, with the flick of the neck. Kevin had to swerve around prostrate bodies of the fallen.

The beast zigzagged through city streets, trouncing over cobblestone ways, brick roads, and dirt paths. Kevin followed in hot pursuit, braking hard, yanking the wheel, anything necessary to keep the chase afoot.

Cunningham tossed about the cabin, trying to steady his rifle, and repeatedly adjusted his helmet. Their circuitous path led downhill, plying toward the great harbor.

Eventually, the Rover rumbled over the Congress Street Bridge, entering South Boston near the Cogeneration Steam Facility. Kevin thought of the intricate clockwork inside the brick building and its peculiar operator, Barnaby Runge.

He began thinking the clockwork had something to do with the bizarre alternate world around him. The intricate cogs seemed more involved than merely providing steam to the city's inhabitants. Something to do with time, or an alternate dimension, he suspected, churned by the unusual gears and sprockets.

Runge ran the facility and maybe a portion of the universe.

A quick turn shook Kevin from his thoughts. The Rhino-pard cut left, plying through thick grass, as it trounced over an open plain.

"The beast is headed toward the docks," Cunningham bellowed.

"I don't trust it," Kevin said, hesitant to pursue.

"Blazes, lad!" Cunningham shook his head. "Get after it."

Kevin stuck to the bumpy roadway. The Rhino-pard dipped into a depression, and a moment later didn't arise on the next knoll. It disappeared from view altogether.

"Where did it go?" Cunningham said agape.

"Running along the depression," Kevin surmised.

"But which direction did it go?"

"Toward the right," Kevin said, pointing at the lowlands.

"What makes you so sure?

"Just don't think that it would double back toward the city."

"The creature does seem bent on pressing toward the shoreline." Cunningham nodded. "Wonder what ails the blasted thing."

Kevin accelerated, trying to get ahead of the beast before the road curved around the end of the open plain. "Look!" he said, pointing.

The Rhino-pard flanked east toward the water. It pounded along a depression, trying to conceal its flight from the hunters. A portion of its rump, and the tip of the horn, bobbed into view sporadically.

"Right you are!" Cunningham yelled.

Stepping on the gas, the Rover accelerated moving ahead of the beast. They were about forty meters to the side of it, traveling along parallel paths. Eventually, the road wound to the left, intersecting with the Rhino-pard's path, and then headed toward the docks where they had started the tracking party.

Kevin pushed the vehicle harder. It swayed to the right as he began cutting around the bend. Cunningham leaned into the passenger door, until the Rover leveled off. Then, he checked over the Weatherby and readied himself to alight the vehicle quickly.

"Once you get to the intersection of that drainage channel," Cunningham barked, "bring her to stop and I'll set up on the hood."

Kevin nodded, thinking the same thing.

As they neared the intersecting point, the Rhino-pard continued charging down the trough. Twenty meters away, Kevin brought the Rover to a stop. Cunningham opened the door as the beast closed the distance by five meters.

Kevin worried the Rhino-pard would merely skirt around them. The beast might keep running along the drainage ditch on the other side of the road. It could be off before Cunningham got into position. He reached for the Ray-gun, and then yanked the door handle on the Rover.

He saw Cunningham leaning over the hood, Weatherby in hand, almost ready to fire. The Great Hunter flicked off the safety as Kevin opened the door. Cunningham's eyes widened and his mouth went agape.

Turning to look, the door slammed shut and Kevin's window shattered. Glass cascaded all over him. He felt the door panel buckle inward, and the Rover lunged into the air.

He grabbed hold of the steering wheel and braced for impact. As the steam vehicle tipped, he caught sight of Cunningham rolling off the hood. The Rover teetered on two wheels for a moment.

Then, Kevin saw the Rhino-pard thump around the front of the vehicle.

A shot rang through the night air. The sound of a big bore rifle echoed in Kevin's ears. And the Rover rattled and creaked, and then dropped hard onto its side.

The windshield cracked; a spider web splintered across the glass. Cunningham let out a cry of pain. Agony. Tearing and shredding sounds emanated from the ground by the hood. A menacing snarl, then heavy thuds padded away toward the ditch.

"Cunningham!" Kevin yelled in panic.

No answer.

The beast got him, ripped the hunter to shreds, Kevin thought. He hung, belted in the driver's seat, with the Rover tipped on the passenger side. His head swirled from blood rushing to his temples, and the sudden loss of equilibrium made him pass out.

CHAPTER TWENTY-FOUR

Entangled in the Rover, Kevin awoke to the sound of rifle fire. He struggled to get loose, while looking for the Ray-gun. Kevin spotted the weapon nestled in the corner of the passenger side floorboards. He stretched and grabbed hold of the handle, and then spun around searching for a way out.

The passenger door was lodged into the roadway, and the driver's door buckled from the blow. He kicked at the windshield with a jackboot, but the glass held strong.

Another shot fired. *The Weatherby*, he thought.

Then he heard a moan.

"Cunningham!" Kevin screamed.

Kevin kicked madly at the glass. It broke and shards fell away. He kicked again and again, dislodging chunks of windshield, making a hole large enough to crawl through.

Broken glass was everywhere, cutting his hands and shredding through the knees of his pants. Adrenaline and anxiety helped mask the pain. He scampered through the shattered windshield and crawled onto the road.

The Great Hunter was sprawled on the cobblestones, a trickle of blood ran from his lip; the Weatherby lay on the deck beside him, bolt open as though getting ready for another shot. A few meters away, the pith helmet sat crushed and marred by a Rhino-pard footprint.

Cunningham groaned.

Kevin rushed to his side, kneeling by the fallen hunter.

"Don't let it get away," Cunningham muttered.

Glancing down the drainage ditch, the Rhino-pard plodded along. Its hind legs kicked up soggy turf. The collision had slowed the beast down, and maybe Cunningham landed a lucky shot. Kevin couldn't fathom ever catching up to the thing on foot.

He rolled Cunningham over and propped him against the grille.

"Tore up my shooting jacket is all," Cunningham said, leaning against the Rover.

Kevin looked at the hunter's chest. The jacket was ripped to shreds and blood oozed from striations, but it wasn't gushing. Superficial wounds, at least to a guy like Cunningham. Kevin thought about going after the beast. Maybe the Rhino-pard would run into a dead end by the water.

Cunningham seemed to sense his thoughts. "Go on, lad," he said. "I'll be quite all right."

Bending over, Kevin snatched up the Weatherby and handed it to Cunningham. "In case it comes back this way," he said.

The Great Hunter nodded, taking the rifle.

Kevin ran across the road and shuffled down the embankment. His shins hurt, but he blocked out the pain. Sprinting along the drainage ditch, he couldn't spot the Rhino-pard ahead. The beasts' tracks were easy to spot, however. He followed churned up mud and bits of grass from its flight.

He clutched the Ray-gun tightly.

The exertion sent his heart racing. Kevin could feel the thrill of the chase mixed with anxiety over another confrontation with the creature. He ran fast, not wanting the beast to get away. At the same time, he dreaded catching up to it.

Cresting a slight incline, a remote edge of the harbor came into view. Kevin saw a narrow service road intersecting with the drainage ditch. A pipe ran beneath the dirt roadway. The Rhino-pard charged up the embankment, and ran across the distant road.

Kevin was less than a hundred meters away.

Beyond the road lay a small point that jutted into the open harbor. The beast was trapped. Kevin eased into a jog, trying to recover some energy.

The creature trampled over the dead grass, headed for the shoreline.

As he neared the service road, Kevin heard an incessant rattling from his left. Cunningham rolled over the service road in a steam jalopy. His chubby cheeks were cast in a sardonic grin.

The Great Hunter seemed oblivious to Kevin's approach. Rumbling over the dirt road, dust kicked up from the jalopy's spoke wheels, then it careened off the roadway into the grass. Cunningham bounced in the seat, keeping to the side of the ditch.

Kevin broke into a sprint. The Rhino-pard swung its head around toward Cunningham. Kevin expected the beast to double back and charge the buggy, but the creature kept pressing for the shoreline.

Cunningham rambled the steam buggy along, driving the beast toward the dock, cutting off any retreat.

Kevin finally saw the beast's destination.

A barge docked at a rickety wharf. The cargo vessel floated offshore, flat, comprised of splintered planks about fifty meters long. A wooden box-container hunkered in the center, and a single line held the barge to the dock, fastened around a pillar.

The Rhino-pard pounded onto the dock. A man stood at the end wearing a top hat and tailcoat. His countenance appeared obtuse in the shadows, but he didn't seem frightened by the stampeding beast.

Then, the Great Hunter wheeled the jalopy around, so the rear-end pointed toward the harbor.

Kevin caught up as Cunningham alighted from the vehicle.

Cunningham trundled around to the back of the buggy, as the beast pounded across the dock. "Don't just stand there, lad!" Cunningham bellowed. "Time is a wasting."

The hunter yanked a tarp off the jalopy. A gleaming brass Gatling gun stood on a tripod. Cunningham had left the buggy idling. There was a hose running from the steam engine to the shiny gun.

"Gas powered by steam?" Kevin asked, helping lower it to the ground.

"Correct indeed, lad," Cunningham replied. "Right you are, once again."

"Where did you get it?" Kevin said, then glanced at the jalopy. "And the steam buggy... where did that come from?"

"Commandeered it along the roadside. An expeditious acquisition."

"You were lying injured by the Rover?"

"They can't keep a good man down long." Cunningham eased the gun around. "No time for talking. Let's get to it."

Kevin understood the Great Hunter had every intention of manning the impressive gun, so he reached for a cartridge belt and began feeding it into the Gatling gun. As soon as the weapon was ready, Cunningham began pulling the trigger.

The barrels pointed slightly downward. Rounds ripped across the dirt roadway, and then tore into the dock. The man with the top hat cackled. Cunningham adjusted the menacing gun on its tripod, as the Rhino-pard thundered into the cargo box.

The man in the top hat stepped onto the barge, dropping the line into murky waters. Another volley of rounds ripped loose. This time, the bullets riddled the end of the dock and found purchase in the barge, strafing planks and blasting into the wooden box-container.

A strong current quickly set the cargo vessel into the harbor. Cunningham let loose, emptying the entire cartridge belt. Bullets stippled the vessel and homed in on the container, but only resulted in jostling the barge when an occasional round struck the Rhino-pard's hide.

"Quick, lad," Cunningham barked. "Reload the gun!"

"Right," Kevin replied, moving surely.

While they prepared for another assault, the man in the top hat closed the box-container door and latched it shut. He turned toward the desperate hunters and bid adieu by tipping his hat and bowing.

"That blasted Frenchman thinks he's going to get away!" Cunningham bellowed.

"The barge is almost out of range, and our rounds are just plugging into waterlogged wood," Kevin said, feeding the gun. "The thing doesn't have a hull to knock a hole into it."

"We'll see about that," Cunningham replied.

The Great Hunter let loose another volley of rounds. The Gatling gun vibrated his hands furiously as the barrels rotated at amazing speed. His chubby face turned red from exhilaration.

Bullets ripped through the deck of the barge and tore into the wooden box-container, but none struck the man in the top hat, and any rounds that pierced the container didn't seem to drop the beast. Kevin only heard the Rhino-pard snort and buck.

Determined, the Great Hunter fired away continuously, until the gun was empty. The last few rounds dropped into the choppy water as the barge drifted out of range.

"Looks like we lost them," Kevin said, stymied.

"Maybe not for long," Cunningham said, pointing.

****

An iron-clad flying the flag of the British Empire trolled toward the barge. The steam-powered military vessel moved at a faster clip than the cargo barge, which had merely been set adrift.

"The Royal Navy will board them soon enough." Cunningham smiled.

A cannon at the bow of the iron-clad erupted. The big gun jolted back, chains rattling, and then a cannonball lobbed through the air. It sailed toward the barge and dropped into the water with a splash. Smoke whisked from the barrel of the cannon.

"Merely a warning shot," Cunningham said.

Kevin smelled the gunpowder wafting through the damp air. The warship seemed to be marking its target as it closed in on the cargo vessel. Another moment and it would be within striking range.

Then, a fog horn blew and an officer opened an iron hatch. He called to the man in the top hat, instructing him to halt the barge.

The Frenchman grinned and extended his hands, palms up, as though implying he didn't have control over his vessel. Kevin knew the Frenchman couldn't steer or slow the barge. The iron-clad closed the distance.

Soon, the iron-clad would pull alongside the barge and marines would fasten lines between the two vessels and board it. Although capture was imminent, the Frenchman didn't appear concerned. In fact, his countenance reflected an aloofness that puzzled Kevin.

Cunningham didn't seem to pick up on the nuance. He stood beside Kevin eagerly, rubbing his hands together, and occasionally bumping his elbow into the young man's arm. "They've about got him," Cunningham jeered. "We'll get the credit for this, instead of the 10th Hussars."

"I've got a funny feeling about this," Kevin said, shaking his head.

"You worry too much, lad," Cunningham reassured him.

"The Frenchman looks too cocky."

"That's his nature. Reality will soon sober his arrogance."

"Not so sure about—"

"What, lad?"

"There is a reason for his pride." Kevin pointed toward the sky.

A massive airship descended from the clouds. It was a full-sized zeppelin with teak wings sprouting from each side. Wooden propellers were strapped under the wings, churning it along with steam power. Hoses ran from the propellers down to a large wooden hull suspended beneath the airship.

The hull was shaped like an early naval warship. Portholes ran along each side with muzzles of big guns poking through the hatches.

"Blazes!" Cunningham bellowed.

As the airship sailed closer to the barge, a long tail-hook swung down from the hull. The Frenchman scurried onto the cargo carrier and picked up a pole. It was the type of rod used by lamplighters for gas lanterns on city streets.

He slid the rod under a coil of rope and then held it high. Thick ropes ran around the cargo carrier.

Another explosion from an iron-clad cannon, and a ball ripped through the deck of the barge. Two more cannon blasts followed. Each resulted in the deck being broken open. A shot splintered into the cargo carrier.

The Rhino-pard bucked inside, desperately trying to break out.

Then, a volley of aerial artillery erupted from the sky. Cannon balls rained down on the iron-clad. The crew scrambled to wheel its cannons back and shut the dense hatches. Lead round shots collided with the iron-plated vessel, denting the armor and then rolling into choppy waters.

A few found purchase at the seams, splintering the wooden support beams inside the vessel. Panels of protective iron gave way and bent inward.

At a break in the fighting, the smell of cordite wafted through the air.

The airship closed in on the barge, hovered, and then gracefully swooped down. The tail-hook caught the bundle of rope and whipped the cargo carrier away.

The wooden carrier swayed back and forth as it rose into the air. Rocking beneath the airship, the Frenchman dropped the pole into the harbor. He stood on top of the cargo carrier and clinched a rope tightly. Then, he smirked at the hunters triumphantly.

Just as the cargo carrier steadied itself, the Frenchman removed his top hat, and gave the hunters a decidedly genteel bow. He stood erect and a button to his tailcoat came undone. A green glow emanated from his torso, revealing a timepiece with Roman numerals housed where the man's stomach should have been.

"Jeepers!" Cunningham barked. "The wag is part steam man."

Kevin didn't quite understand, but he remained silent. He wasn't sure if he wanted to know. They stood quietly, watching the airship get smaller in the moonlight. The only sound came from distant grumblings of the crew on the iron-clad.

CHAPTER TWENTY-FIVE

Standing on the platform at North Station, Kevin looked over his comrades with mixed emotions. He wore the civilian clothes of his time. Kevin desperately wanted to get back home to his parents and the life that he knew. But part of him wanted to stay, and join in the next adventure.

Sarah stood beside Cunningham, looking elegant in her Victorian attire. Her dress was black and silky with a bright pink liner that folded in front, revealing her bosom. Kevin longed to be with her.

The Great Hunter smiled and clapped him on the shoulder. "You did a great job, lad. Showed a lot of courage. I knew you had it in you all along."

"Thank you, sir," Kevin replied. "Just wish we could've gotten both of them."

"Nonsense. We'll keep after the Frenchman," Cunningham said, adjusting his Australian bush hat. "Don't *you* worry about it a moment longer."

"Wish that I could join you. Seems like we made a great team."

"No need to worry," Niles interjected from a rustic wheelchair. "You went above and beyond. I'll never forget that night when you got the flare off in time for me to fire up the cogeneration plant."

Glancing at Niles in the wheelchair, oak boards and rattan seating, Kevin noticed the front wheels were the size of bicycle tires and the rear wheels were significantly smaller, basically the reverse of what you'd find in Kevin's world. The difference made him understand that it was time to get back to his old life.

He gave Sarah a kiss on the cheek, then picked up his portmanteau. He bid adieu to the others and headed for the train.

"Keep hunting!" Cunningham said, tipping his hat.

Kevin felt a tinge of anxiety and couldn't look back. The pain at leaving them forever was unbearable. He hustled down the platform, and then rushed up a set of stairs to board the train. He shoved the portmanteau into the overhead. Nestling into a plush leather window seat, he finally turned toward his friends.

The sendoff party began to break up. Cunningham spun the wheelchair around and pushed Niles away. While the two plodded off, Sarah stood watching the train, as though trying to determine where Kevin had sat down.

She finally locked glances with him and waved cheerfully.

A tear ran down his cheek. He waved back and hoped she hadn't noticed. The sorrow he felt came as much from the thought of leaving her forever, as the lack of remorse that she exhibited. *Perhaps she doesn't reciprocate my feelings*, he thought.

He waved to her again, then wiped his cheek and faced forward. The train began to chug, and he hoped that it was only a matter of time before it transformed into a commuter rail.

As the train slowly eased out of North Station, he noticed a man sitting across the aisle, familiar.

Kevin couldn't recall where he'd seen the man. The fellow dressed in Victorian work clothes, wool knickers, and a white shirt with suspenders.

A conductor approached wearing a fine wool uniform. He asked to see Kevin's ticket and punched a hole in it. Then, the conductor turned and faced the man across the aisle. The stranger didn't have a ticket and seemed to be struggling to pull out enough money for the fare. That's when Kevin recognized him as the freeloader from the inbound train.

"We're not going to have the likes of you aboard this train," the conductor said in a heavy brogue. He pulled a cord and the train lurched to a halt.

The man appeared desperate.

"Off you go," the conductor said, pointing toward a door.

"He can have my ticket," Kevin said, handing it over. He grabbed the portmanteau and alighted from the train.

Kevin ran down the platform, gripping his leather bag. He noticed for the first time, a faded stamp on the side of the leather bag, the seal of the Royal Society of Steam Engineers. He glanced back at the train and saw Roland in a wool suit, smiling from ear-to-ear.

The crowds sending off their loved ones had disbursed. Sarah stood alone on the platform facing away from him, sobbing.

He bounded up to Sarah and flung her around. She was halfway into a roundhouse punch when she registered him. Her face lit up into a smile.

"We're going to have great adventures together," Sarah said coolly.

Kevin kissed Sarah and then held her in a firm embrace. Letting her go, they walked down the platform hand-in-hand toward the Rover. He couldn't wait to see the looks on the hunters' faces.

THE END

John W. Dennehy is a writer of Horror & Suspense. His first book Clockwork Universe is out now from Severed Press. He has two more books expected from Severed Press in 2017, including Pacific Rising and Deepwater Drift. His stories have appeared in SQ Mag, Disturbed Digest, Typehouse Literary Magazine, Beyond Science Fiction, and in anthologies such as Winter Shivers, Bones III, and SNAFU: Wolves at the Door, and many others. Currently, he is working on a Supernatural Horror novel.

After graduating from Pinkerton Academy, he enlisted in the U.S. Marines, serving with MALS-26 Patriots. Then John earned a degree in English/Creative Writing at UNC Wilmington. John is a member of HWA, MWA, and NEHW. He lives in New England and can be found at http://johnwdennehy.com/.